The English Rebels

FRANCES MARY

ISBN 979-8-89243-470-6 (paperback)
ISBN 979-8-89243-471-3 (digital)

Christian Faith Publishing
832 Park Avenue
Meadville, PA 16335
www.christianfaithpublishing.com

Printed in the United States of America

Joan was born in London and grew up there until she was fourteen. In furious escape, she accidentally boarded a ship bound for America with her twelve-year-old brother. Being adopted by the kindly captain, Joan and her brother slowly learn what trust means. Later, when Joan and her brother discover they have a wealthy uncle who has been searching for them, they travel to New York to find him. But with the advancing danger of the coming war, Joan has some big decisions to make.

Chapter 1

Joan stared with wide eyes at the long column of red-coated soldiers as they passed by her. She turned to her brother, Jamerson. Two years younger than her, at age twelve, he stood with his blue eyes large. He was a stolid little soul with broad shoulders for his years and reddish-colored hair, so rare that Joan had never seen another person with that shade of hair. It was as though it had its own lights because it always seemed to catch the light and seemed to burn a fire red. Joan was terribly protective of him because they had no parents, and she had raised him from when he had been only five. They had lived in corners where people didn't notice them, and she had begged until she could work. They lived in London, England, and it was the year 1772. These soldiers were parading down the wharf and getting onto a warship that would take them across the ocean to the far-off land of America.

"You know," Jamerson whispered, watching them, "I don't like it. Somehow I don't want them to win!"

Joan smiled down at him. "I know, but we best get going. I've got work to get back to."

Jamerson smiled. "Alright." Together, they weaved through the madly shouting crowd, and Joan hurried back toward the baker's shop.

"Now remember, you must stay hidden until I come back. After all, you know that the policemen are gathering up orphans and taking them to those awful convents!" It wasn't a threat but a fact, and Jamerson understood and took her warning.

Joan slipped into the kitchen, and the chief baker looked up. "There you are, and just in time. I need you to carry more flour in." Joan nodded and hurried to the storeroom. She picked up the heavy bag of flour and carried it into the kitchen. "Good. Now," the baker said. "Now the front is a bit overcrowded. Hurry in and help Joseph with the customers." Joan nodded again. She hurried to the sales counter and began to take orders. With her and the baker's son, Joseph, selling the bread as fast as they could, the shop soon emptied. He flashed her a grateful smile before hurrying to refill the trays. Joan then had to hurry back to the kitchen to bring in more eggs and milk and de-stem the berries for the bakery's famous berry tarts. She worked hard.

Finally, the long day was over, and the shop closed. But though it was closed, that didn't mean Joan's job was done. She washed down the stove and tables, did the mountain of dishes, swept and mopped the floor, and cleaned the front of the bakery. By then, it was nigh onto midnight, and the long-tired day was over. She stripped off her dirty apron and hurried out, locking the door behind her. She made her way to the poor quarters of a very old apartment building, in which she and Jamerson shared a room that she paid for. Seven long flights of stairs she climbed. Jamerson was sleeping when she came in, so she slipped into her pile of rags and fell instantly asleep.

The next morning, at five o'clock, Joan dragged herself up. She crept over to Jamerson's side to make sure he was alright then left the room silently. In an alley behind the apartment building, and in the dim light of the still-burning street lamps, she washed her face and hands. She undid her hair and re-braided it, straightening her unruly curls the best she could with her fingers. Then she started out toward the bakery. The baker's wife was stirring up the fire when Joan entered. She nodded solemnly toward her, and then the day began.

Joan carried in the ingredients to make the bread and pasties. Both she and the baker's wife worked, making fresh bread for the day. Both were still too tired to say much. But at seven o'clock, the baker entered and opened the shop. All day long, Joan worked like she had every day since she had gotten the job a year earlier. It was again midnight before she had finished cleaning up and crept home.

Jamerson was again asleep. He was what pushed her on, what made it so that after four hours of sleep, she would get up and go back to work. On Sunday, the two children got some time together. That was when Joan and Jamerson traveled about London and wandered the public gardens together, and Joan washed the very few garments they owned. They both had baths so that they could at least feel human.

On a Sunday, Joan awoke at seven, glad of the sleep-in. A few wet splotches on the floor showed that it had rained during the night. But the sun was up, and she climbed to her feet and sighed contentedly. Like always, she would hurry and take her bath before Jamerson got up and then tackle the wash so it would dry while they wandered the city. An hour later, Joan had done just that, and Jamerson awoke to take his bath and pass out his dirty clothes to her from behind the ragged sheet that screened the tub from view. "I can hardly wait to take a walk this morning," he called. "The place will be just buzzing." Joan laughed; her own blood quickened with excitement. Something told her that today would be something to be remembered.

Jamerson jammed his fists deeper into his pockets and leaned back on the park bench. He squinted through the tree branches overhead. "The sky is so blue today," Joan said drowsily.

"Joan, look, a policeman. He's walking toward us." Joan opened one eye. Yes, there was a policeman walking down the path toward them.

"We're just two children enjoying a day in the park," Joan said quietly under her breath, calming Jamerson.

The policeman stopped before them. "Now you two," he said, holding his club in both hands. "What may a pair of two youngsters be doing in a park alone?"

"Just taking a walk," Joan said quietly.

"Where be your parents?" the policeman asked.

"Well…um…we…a…" Joan stammered, groping for the right words. "Th…they're in church."

The policeman nodded slowly. "And why mightn't you be there too?"

"We…a…" She stopped, then said in a rush, "We didn't want to go."

The policeman raised a brow. "Well, now I guess I'll just have to take you to your parents."

Joan looked frantically at Jamerson. "They'll give us a good hard thrashing, policeman. Please don't take us back," said Jamerson, coming to her rescue.

"Well, now I'll just talk to them," said the policeman.

"Now come along." Joan looked desperately for a way out, but there was none.

Chapter 2

It's all my fault! It's all my fault! Joan thought, standing in front of the desk where a nun with a round and plump face sat.

"Names, children?" she asked solemnly.

"Joan and Jamerson," Joan said softly.

A heavy lump in her throat made it hard to speak. "Joan and Jamerson what?" asked the nun, holding a quill poised over a paper.

"Just Joan and Jamerson," Joan said softly.

"Hmm," the nun said and wrote down their names. "Now you go along. Sister Donna will show you to your rooms." Joan looked at

5

the tall and thin nun that stood beside the door of the office. As she hurried out of the room, her eyes flicked about, searching desperately for an escape route. But there was none.

A week and two days later, Joan and Jamerson had been in the convent when Sister Hannah, the convent's head nun, called them to her office. There, a man and woman waited with the nun. "What a beautiful boy!" said the woman, coming over to Jamerson. He took a step back. The woman smiled. "Shy, isn't he? We'll take him, Sister." The nun nodded.

"Wait," Jamerson said. "What about my sister?" He nodded toward Joan. The woman looked at Joan for the first time.

"Well," she said slowly. "I already have a daughter. I just want a son."

Joan straightened her shoulders. "We stay together," she said quietly.

"Joan, if you can't mind your manners, you can leave the room," Sister Hannah said.

Joan only nodded. "Where will you take him, so I can write?" Joan asked.

The woman thought then handed her a small, delicate card that had her address on it. "Now come along, Jamerson."

Jamerson pulled back. "No," he said.

"Jamerson, come along!" said the woman, taking his hand, but Jamerson shook his head and planted his feet firmly.

"No, I'm staying with Joan."

"Jamerson!" said Sister Hannah.

The woman began to drag Jamerson from the room. "Joan!" he cried.

Joan jumped forward. For his cries were all she could stand. "Let him go!" she cried, trying to pry the woman's fingers off Jamerson's wrist. Sister Hannah jerked her back. "Let me go!" Joan cried, struggling with everything she had.

"Hold still, child!" Sister Hannah hissed.

"Joan!" Jamerson cried, catching the door jamb of the office and holding on tightly.

"Jamerson, I'm coming!" Joan said. She kicked Sister Hannah in the shin, and the nun's grip on her loosened. Joan bolted forward. She began to pry the woman's fingers off Jamerson's wrist and had almost succeeded when Sister Donna and Sister Hannah both pulled her back, holding her firmly between them. "Jamerson!" Joan cried as the woman began to drag him toward the front door.

"Joan!" Jamerson cried, pulling back. "Let me loose!" Tears were flooding down Joan's cheeks as she struggled to free herself. "Joan!" Jamerson cried again, just before the front door banged behind the man and woman. Joan watched through the window as they put him in a carriage, and it drove away. Only after the big iron gates had closed did the nuns let her go, and then Joan streaked out the door and to the gates. But only the gatekeeper could open them. Joan tried, but through the bars, she could see the carriage driving away and Jamerson's face in the small window at the back.

Joan couldn't eat or sleep. Jamerson was gone. She didn't cry anymore, but her mind worked hard, trying to figure out a way to leave the convent and get to him. Then, one day, she got it. A boy about her own age was leaving for another convent some miles away. Joan had an idea, and she approached him one day as he was working in the gardens. She had only one valuable possession, and she had carried it around with her since her parents had died. It was a gold and silver brooch of her mother's. She had hidden it on the inside of her shabby dress. Now she held the brooch in her hand. "Samuel," she said quietly. "Do you want to earn this?" He stared down at the brooch. Then nodded. "Borrow me some garments and let me go to that other convent," Joan said.

"What? Are you crazy?" Samuel asked.

"Maybe, but that is how you can earn this."

Samuel looked at the brooch and then said quietly, "Alright."

With Samuel's hat tipped low over her forehead, Joan looked like one of the band of boys that climbed into the wagon to be driven to the other convent. Two nuns sat in the wagon to make sure none of them tried to escape. Outside the convent, Joan bided her time. After they had traveled about a mile, she shoved one of the boys hard against one nun. "Hey, what's the big idea!" he shouted as he crashed into the nun.

"What's going on?" asked the other nun.

Joan shoved another boy at her. "So help me!" He whirled and swung a punch at her. She ducked, and it hit the boy behind her in the nose. Instantly, the wagon was in an uproar. The nuns were so busy trying to stop the other boys fighting that they didn't notice Joan slip off the wagon and dart down a side street. Now she drew the card from her pocket as she ran, looked at the address, and then ran on.

Joan stood before the door, her hat pulled down over her forehead. She had rung the bell, and now the door opened. "Yes?" asked a man in a black coat and breeches. "I have a message here for a boy named Jamerson," she said in a low voice, like a boy's.

"Oh?" the man asked. "Then come right in. The lad hasn't been feeling that good, so you can't see him, but can I take a message?"

"Sure," Joan said, keeping her voice low. The man led her into a library to the right and nodded toward a table that had a quill and ink. Joan didn't have good handwriting, but she had learned to read and write some. So she scribbled.

> *Have you ever heard the book of Joan of Arc?*
> *If you want the book of Joan then meet me at the*
> *fountain out front at three o'clock, and I'll take you*
> *to see your friend.*

Hopefully, he would get the hint. She didn't bother to fold it and held it out toward the man, saying in a low voice, "The boy loves books, and he has a bookkeeper as a friend that lets him take books." The man nodded and took the paper.

Joan stood beside the fountain and waited. Just when she was about to give up and think that Jamerson hadn't gotten the hint, the door opened, and he came down the stairs and over to her. She knew he didn't recognize her and was glad. "Come along," she said in a low voice. Then out of sight from the house, she said in her own voice, "Now let's run!"

"Joan!" Jamerson cried. Joan smiled. "I'm glad you came," Jamerson said as the two ran through the crowd and toward the wharf. "Hey," Jamerson whispered, "let's sneak aboard a ship bound for America." Joan looked at him, then at the ships in the harbor, and then out toward the ocean. Her mind flew back through the years of dodging the policemen and convents. They surely wouldn't have convents in America, and she and Jamerson could stay together. She frowned, but what would happen to them in this strange new land?

"Hey, you!" a voice suddenly shouted, and Joan and Jamerson flipped around. It was the same policeman who had caught them before.

"Run!" Jamerson yelled, and the two streaked down the wharf, weaving in and out of piles of crates, people, and barrels.

"Stop those two boys!" the policeman yelled as he started after them. Joan and Jamerson ran side by side. They didn't know where they were running, and before they could really tell where they were going, they had run aboard a ship. Before anyone could see them, they slipped down into the hold and hid among the barrels and crates.

"Who's there?" a gruff voice asked, but they only crouched lower, and nothing happened. They listened while more stuff was loaded into the hold and then heard a far-off shout from overhead, "Pull in the gangplank!" They held their breath. They waited a few more hours and then crept out of their hiding places. They went up the ladder and peeked out of the hatchway. The sky was dark and cloudless, speckled with millions of stars.

"There are way more stars than in London," Jamerson whispered.

"Yeah, I wonder where we're going." They crept up a few more rungs on the ladder so that their heads came out of the hole. Two sailors stood watch, but they didn't notice them. Joan looked over at Jamerson, and he grinned. Her heart beat wildly. She had heard stories of stowaways and wondered what would happen to them if they were ever found out. She climbed back down the ladder. Jamerson followed. "I'm hungry," he whispered to her.

"I know, but there is nothing to eat." She sat down behind some barrels. "Let's get some sleep." Jamerson nodded and sat down beside her.

Chapter 3

Joan awoke first, her stomach telling her she hadn't eaten for almost twenty-four hours, but she was worried about Jamerson. She looked around then slowly got up. There was only one way she could think of. She went to the hatchway ladder. Slowly, she climbed up. Her whole body was shaking with fear, but she gulped and pulled down her hat tighter. The hatchway door had been closed, and she pushed at it. It wasn't locked. Slowly, with all her strength, she pushed it open and peeked out. She found ten pairs of eyes watching her. One man in a blue coat strode forward. "Boy," he bellowed. "What's the meaning of sneaking onto my ship?"

Joan gulped and then lowered her voice. "We didn't mean to. It's just that the police were chasing us, and we only intended to hide for a while until we were in the clear, but you left the harbor too soon."

The man looked angry. "We?" he asked. "You mean there is more than one of you?"

Joan gulped. "Y…yes, sir, my little brother, but please, sir, don't punish him. He's only twelve, and I'm fully responsible for this."

The man glowered at her. "If you were older, I'd throw you overboard, but since you're not, you'll work out your passage."

Joan sighed with relief. "Yes, sir." She looked at him. "I said I would take full responsibility. I'll take my share and my brother's." The captain crossed his arms and raised an eyebrow. He had red, bushy hair and a beard, so he looked fierce.

"Oh, will you?" he asked.

"Yes, sir."

"And what do you expect to happen to your brother?"

She thought then said, "Teach him to be a sailor."

The captain's beard twitched.

"Teach him to be a sailor?" he asked. "Yes, sir."

The captain looked around at his crew. "What do you think, lads?"

he asked. "We'll teach the lad if this one here wants to take his work for as long as he will."

Joan nodded. "I will."

A few of the men grinned, and the captain held out his hand. "It's a deal," he said. "Now go get that kid brother of yours."

Joan hurried back down into the hold. Jamerson was still sleeping, and she awoke him. "What is it?" he asked when she woke him. "The captain wants to meet you. He thinks I'm a boy, and I'll tell him my name is Joe. You must remember to call me that also, or you could put us in danger." Jamerson's eyes were large, but he nodded and followed her up the hatchway and onto the deck. "The captain and his crew will teach you to be a sailor," Joan told him, and his eyes grew huge.

*****

"This is my brother, Jamerson," Joan told the captain. He looked at Jamerson with one eyebrow raised.

"Humph!" he said then turned to one of his men. "You're in charge of him. Teach him everything you can until the trip is finished."

Joan looked up at the captain. "Sir, where are we bound for?"

"America," the captain said, and then, "Your first job is to swab down the deck."

A week passed, and Joan worked harder than she had ever worked. Blisters became a thing hardly noticed. But watching Jamerson's delight in getting to learn to be a sailor was pay enough. It also made it easier to work. She swabbed down the deck daily and helped the cook with numerous odd jobs, not counting the ones that every sailor on the ship had for her. One day, about halfway through their voyage, a large storm came upon the ship. When the captain yelled for all hands on deck, the sailor on tend Jamerson said to him, "Come on, kid!"

Joan jumped to her feet. "He can't go up there!" she said in her boy voice.

"Look, I'm on tend him so I tell him what he's supposed to do," said the sailor.

"It's alright, Joe. I want to go," Jamerson said.

Joan waited for a few minutes after they had left, then went on deck. The wind was blowing terribly, and the ocean rocked around her. She looked around. Just as she looked up, she saw Jamerson fall from the rigging where he was clinging.

"Jamerson!" Joan screamed, forgetting that she was supposed to be a boy. She saw him fall into the icy waters. She ran to the side of the ship.

"Joan!" Jamerson screamed. He was in the water a few yards from the ship and getting carried away.

"I'm coming, Jamerson!" Joan screamed and grabbed the end of a rope nearby. She threw one end to another sailor, and then, with the other end in both hands, she jumped overboard. She knew how to swim, but her light body was no match for the raging ocean. But struggling and praying hard, she reached Jamerson. She passed the rope into his hands. "Pull!" she screamed above the roar of the storm. The sailors on board began to pull. Joan held onto the rope too. A few minutes later, they were dragged aboard. Joan didn't even stop to think but knelt by Jamerson's side. "Jamerson, are you alright?" she asked.

He groaned and then coughed. "Joan," he muttered. "I thought you'd never come."

Joan coughed softly, then said, "I'm going to get you down below." She helped him to his feet and then helped him down to his cabin.

Two hours later, the storm had blown itself out, and Jamerson had fallen asleep, so Joan went on deck. The sun had risen, so she started to swab down the deck. She had just started when she heard the captain's voice. "Hey, Joe." She looked up. "Or is it Joan?" he said, watching her closely.

Joan stared at him with wide eyes. "How did you know?" she asked.

The captain nodded slowly. "Why didn't you tell me you were a girl?" he asked.

Joan looked down. "You never asked," she said as she shoved the swab around and around in little circles.

"If you're a girl, why did you bargain to take on both yours and your brother's work?"

Joan shrugged. "I don't know. He wanted to be a sailor, and why should I take that away from him when he could learn?"

The captain snorted. "He doesn't know why you're working your insides out from sun up until sun down. He just thinks you like that."

Joan nodded. "I do if it means bringing happiness to him," she said slowly.

The captain snorted again. "Females! Humph!" And he marched off, muttering to himself. Joan smiled and returned to her work.

Chapter 4

After that, the work eased, and Joan was even taught a little about being a sailor. Then came the day when there was a holler from the rigging. "Land! Land ahead!" Joan rushed to the rail, her eyes searching the horizon. For a moment, she could see nothing, and then a very thin line of shore appeared. America! Was it really only two months since she had boarded this ship in flight? Now here she stood, the salt wind blowing steadily against her face.

"Joan, do you see it?" Jamerson hollered, running up. He wore a shirt a size too big for him, dark blue, and a pair of loose jeans held up by a rope around his middle, tied tightly. His red hair was ruffled from the wind and filled with saltwater spray.

"Yes, I see it. Isn't it wonderful!"

Jamerson laughed, his blue eyes bright. "You haven't even seen it really."

Joan smiled. "So? It's a free land. *Free.*" She breathed the words with reverence and then turned toward Jamerson. "What will we do there?"

Jamerson shrugged. "I intend to keep working here if the captain will have me."

Joan stared at him. "But that will mean going to and fro!"

Jamerson grinned. "I know. Imagine the places we'll see."

"Not *we*, Jamerson."

He stared at her. "The captain would never take me on his own free will, not a girl. Sailors think girls are bad luck."

Jamerson waved it off. "Pash! That's poppycock!" Then he bolted off, whistling a boisterous melody the sailors had taught him.

Joan watched him go with a lump in her throat. When the time came, would he choose her or the ship he loved?

That night, restless and worried, Joan went on deck. The ship was moving toward land steadily on the soft breeze. She stood at the rail, watching the approaching shore. There it stood now on two sides of her. She had mixed emotions about that distant shore, feeling excitement and dread.

There was a heavy footstep, and Joan looked up. It was Jerry, the first mate. He was a broad Swede with blond hair and blue eyes, standing a whole three feet above her. He was about thirty, his face hardened by years on the seas. "What's the matter, lass?" he asked, bending down to rest his elbows on the deck railing. Joan looked up at him.

A slight smile twisted her lips. "Ah, nothing really."

Jerry looked out across the water toward the shore. "America, ah, a sweet sight. What are you going to do once you get there?"

Joan looked up at him again. "I don't know. It really depends on Jamerson."

Jerry looked down at her. "Eh? How's that?" Joan looked carefully out toward the shore.

"Do you think the captain would take me on the ship?"

Jerry sighed heavily, and she looked back at him. "Na, lass. I'm afraid not. He thinks lasses and women are bad luck. Won't even take his own wife on voyages. Not that she'd like to either," he said.

Joan sighed. "And Jamerson?"

"Jamerson. Well, the lad's proved to be a true sailor. Has a keen sense of direction and a smart head and hands. The captain, well, he'll take him on if he wants to stay."

Joan nodded softly. "Aye. That he will."

Jerry looked down at her. "You're his sister. What are you going to do?"

Joan sighed softly. "You know, it's hard to say this, but perhaps this will be the best for him. I've raised him the best I can, but he needs a man in his life. A boy just can't be raised by his sister." She clasped her hands together before her on the rail. "Me, well, I might stick around and see him when he comes back to harbor."

"You could make him leave," Jerry said quietly.

Joan looked up and shook her head. "No, Jerry. His heart is on the ship. Why would I take him away from it? He loves the ocean, and who knows, he might become a great merchant someday. Or a great discoverer," she said softly. "Who knows?" she said again quietly. Then she turned. "Well, goodnight, Jerry. See you in the morning." Then she climbed down the hatchway and made her way to her cabin.

*****

"Coming into harbor!" The bellow awoke Joan. She sat straight up in bed. For a moment, she sat there then scrambled out and up to the deck.

"Look, Joan! Look!" Jamerson called. Joan walked over. Yes, the harbor was nothing like London. In fact, there wasn't even one other ship, but a small crowd had gathered on the small wharf. The captain guided the ship safely into the harbor, and two sailors jumped to the wharf to secure it. Joan stood apart while the supplies from the hold were unloaded. Jamerson worked alongside the sailors. Joan stood back and watched him. Yes, he was happy.

Now she had to leave. She went down to her cabin. She cleaned it the best she could and pulled on her hat. Her cut hair had grown some so that it now hung to her shoulders. She tied it back with a thick cord. She had no luggage, so she had best get going. As she came on deck, she noticed that the crowd had mostly drifted away, and Jerry was locking up the hold. Joan looked around her. Then she called to Jerry. He looked up and then walked over. "I think I'll go ashore now," she said quietly without looking up.

"Aren't you going to say goodbye to your brother?"

Joan shook her head. "No, goodbyes weren't made for Jamerson."

"Joan! Hey, Joan!" Jamerson suddenly called, running along the deck toward her.

"The captain says he wants to take us home and meet his family."

Joan smiled. "Very well." She followed him to the gangplank.

Chapter 5

The town was nothing to brag about: one or two shops and a huddle of box-like houses, about twenty of them, and a meetinghouse. The captain led Jamerson and Joan along a street to one of these houses, where white roses and pink daisies grew by the door. As they were coming up the path, the door opened, and a plump woman with dark auburn hair cried, "James!" She hurried out to meet them. "Kurt isn't yet home from his lessons," she told the captain. Then she looked at Joan and Jamerson. "Who are these two lads, James?" she asked her husband.

"No, Martha, one lad and one girl. Stowaways that I found on my ship."

The woman stared at them. "A girl! Let me guess, the older one is the girl."

The captain nodded. "Aye, Martha, and I wouldn't have taken her on except that I didn't find out she was a girl until it was too late to turn back."

"I should have known," said the woman good-naturedly. "She's too pretty to be a boy." She smiled. "Now come on in," she said to them all.

Inside, there was a large room to one side of the door, in which was a large fireplace that almost filled one whole wall. On the hearth were pots, kettles, and pans. Shelves around the room were filled with household items. From the rafters hung bundles of spices and herbs. Before the fire stood a large table set with six chairs, and near the door was a cupboard filled with fine china dishes. The floor was made of planks sanded down to make a smooth surface. The front door opened onto a quite small entry with the big room off to the right and a closed door to the left. Straight before the door was a narrow staircase. "Come on in and get a bite to eat," said the woman, leading them into the big room. "I have some chicken stewing and some corn pudding in the pot." She set out some dishes, and the three sat down.

Joan ate but little. They were halfway through the meal when the front door banged, and then she heard footsteps enter the entry, and she looked up. A tall boy who seemed too skinny for his wiry frame stood in the door. His hair was a dark coppery brown. His eyes were like his mother's, a dark sea-greenish/grayish. He stopped in the doorway for an instant, then grinned at his father. "I'm glad to see you, Father." He came over to shake his father's hand.

"Good to see you, son," the captain said, standing up.

"I didn't think you'd be in for another week or so," said the boy.

"Well, we had good weather this trip and made it in early. I'd like you to meet Jamerson and Joan."

The boy looked over at them. "How do you do?"

Joan caught the surprise that crossed his face when the captain introduced her as a girl. She nodded, mute and too shy to say anything. She was always shy around strangers.

But Jamerson grinned. "I'm glad to meet you," he said.

"I'm glad you're here, Kurt, because I have a question that concerns us all." Martha brought Kurt some food and then sat down. "So when I took Jamerson and Joan on, I did it because I didn't know Joan was a girl. Now if I'd thought ahead to their future, I would have turned back right then. But since I didn't, I guess I found myself two foster children if…" he nodded to his son and wife, "…you agree."

Martha smiled as she looked at Joan. "Of course. Joan here can take Eliza's old place." And her eyes clouded ever so slightly.

"I don't mind," Kurt said. "Jamerson could share a room with me."

The captain nodded and turned to Joan and Jamerson. "How do you two feel about it?"

Jamerson grinned broadly. "I wouldn't mind."

All eyes turned to Joan, who sat with downcast eyes. "If…if we're not intruding," she said quietly.

"You're not, dear," said Martha quietly.

"Then it's settled. Jamerson, you will attend school with Kurt until you're of age, then I can take you on board my ship." Jamerson's eyes widened.

"But I thought…"

The captain smiled. "No, Jamerson. You'll have to have your schooling first. By the way, Kurt, how is your schooling?"

Kurt smiled slightly. "As dull as ever, but I'm happy to announce I'll be out next year."

His father clapped him on the shoulder. "That's fine, son."

"Then can I come aboard with you?" asked Kurt.

His father grinned. "That you can, son," he said.

"When I'm done with my schooling, can I come aboard too?" Jamerson asked eagerly. The captain smiled. "If you must."

Jamerson beamed his pleasure.

*****

19

"This was my daughter Eliza's room. She would have been just your age," said Martha, holding the candle high so that its light fell into the corners of the small room. Joan stood in the doorway looking at the still room. At one end of the room, the chimney from the fireplace below filled the whole end of the room. About three feet away stood a bed. At the foot of the bed was a trunk. Behind the door stood a row of pegs. Beside the bed, on the side closest to the door, was a small night table with strange objects on it. Martha moved to the trunk and opened the lid. "Come, dear," she said quietly and set the candle on the floor beside her. Joan went quietly into the room and knelt beside her. Martha lifted out a piece of cloth from the trunk, which turned out to be a dress of a bluish-greenish color. "This will match your eyes," said Martha with a smile. "It will be so good to have a daughter in the house again."

Joan reached out and touched the dress softly with a forefinger, as though afraid to damage it. Martha laid it on the bed. Then she began to unpack the trunk of its belongings: two more dresses, snow-white petticoats, underclothes, and a soft nightgown. To a girl who had spent her life in ragged clothes, sleeping and working in them alike, this was heaven.

"So this will be your room," Martha said to her at last, sitting back on her heels. "You'll have to keep it neat and clean." Joan nodded without saying a word. "Now come along before it is too late to take your bath." An hour later, Joan lay in bed, staring at the ceiling with wide eyes. This was the first time she had slept in a real bed. She thought she couldn't sleep, but she found she could, and she did.

The next thing Joan knew, Martha was shaking her shoulder. "Joan, wake up." Joan sat up. She saw Martha's face in the light of the candle and remembered where she was. She swung her legs out of bed, and Martha turned to go, then stopped. "Joan, where is the mirror?" she asked, looking at the nightstand.

"Mirror?" Joan repeated blankly.

"Yes, the mirror that was sitting on the nightstand."

Joan frowned. "Is that her name?" she asked.

"Whose name?" asked Martha, perfectly perplexed.

"The name of that head sitting on my nightstand. It gave me the perfect creeps. After all, no head can fit into something so thin!" Joan said as she pulled on a dress.

"You mean…?" Martha asked, and then her mouth twitched at the corners. "Where did you put 'her'?" she asked. Joan knelt by the bed and brought out the mirror, face down.

Martha took it, a soft giggle escaping her. "Joan, this is a mirror. It gives you a reflection of yourself. See?" She turned the mirror toward herself.

"It is my face in it now?" Joan's eyes lit up. "Ohh," she cried. Martha handed back the mirror. Joan peered into the mirror. "So that's me?" she asked. From the mirror looked back at a pair of eyes that were the color of turquoise, fringed by long and thick black lashes. Softly curly golden locks of hair fell back from a softly oval face that was slightly tan and had wind-reddened cheeks.

Martha laughed. "Yep."

Joan wrinkled her nose. "It still gives me the creeps." Then she laid the mirror on the nightstand and brushed back her hair. Drawing it high up onto her head, she tied a ribbon tightly around it and then pulled on a cap. Now she looked like a regular girl.

Chapter 5

◆◇◆

Martha soon realized that Joan would do any job; none was too hard, too dirty, or too tiresome. Also, her reading and writing weren't good, but they weren't bad either. She was willing to learn and took everything with a bright smile. Soon, her cooking skills had excelled almost every other girl in town her own age. Her sewing, as Martha found out, was quite good. But though Martha knew, Joan did not. She was only trying her best to make herself useful, and all she cared about was her and Jamerson being together.

Joan sat at the table shelling peas. Her hair had grown longer after two months of being at the Hoods, which, by the way, was the captain's last name. It now hung halfway to her elbows. She had removed her cap and shook it back to let the air get to it because it was hot, for it was now July. It was about time Jamerson and Kurt were getting home from school. Joan had dinner almost ready, besides a few things. Martha had gone to take a pattern to her friend. The door opened, and Jamerson and Kurt came in, talking just a bit loudly. The two boys came into the kitchen. Joan looked up. She was still quiet and shy; she had kept mostly to herself.

"Joan, I'm starving!" Jamerson said and plopped down on the bench, reaching out to pick at the peas. Joan smiled as though to say, "You're a growing boy," and nodded toward a plate of small corn cakes at the end of the table and a pitcher of milk. The boys sat down and, while they ate the corn cakes and milk, continued to talk. Joan listened.

"I say what them folks in Rhode Island did was what them blasted Redcoats deserved!" Kurt said, biting off the edge of his cake. He chuckled, "I sure wish I could have seen the face of that *Lieutenant William Duddington* when John Brown and his fellows got aboard that ship of his, the *Gaspee*."

Jamerson took a swallow of milk. "What happened?" He asked around another bite of cake. Kurt grinned as though the very thought of it made the blood beat with excitement. "One of the captains out of Newport led him on a merry chase, and Duddington ran aground. Well, news quickly reached Providence, and a party of fifty-five, led by John Brown, planned an attack on the ship. The following evening, they surrounded and boarded the *Gaspee*, wounding Duddington and capturing the entire crew. All were hauled ashore and abandoned, to watch as the *Gaspee* was looted and then burned." He snickered. "Duddington and crew were able to point out most of the participants readily."

Jamerson's face grew tense. "Did they get arrested?"

Kurt grinned. "Nope, because the local courts weren't real fond of the Royal Navy themselves. Instead of prosecuting the attackers, charges were brought against Lt. Duddington for illegally seizing goods from other ships."

Jamerson grinned, his eyes sparkling. "I wish I could have been there," he said and swallowed the last bite of cake.

"But you're English yourself," said Kurt.

"Aw, not really. Joan told me once that our father once said we came from Sweden."

Joan looked up and smiled softly. "Switzerland," she corrected.

"Oh yeah, well," Jamerson said, standing up.

Right then, the door opened, and Martha came in. "I'm glad you're here, boys." She smiled. "Hurry with your chores before dinner is ready."

*****

"Joan, dear, you've been working hard all morning," Martha said as she straightened and laid a hand on the small of her back. "Why don't you take a rest?"

Joan looked up from where she knelt on the floor, scrubbing the boards. "I must finish up here."

"Yes, I know, but after, why don't you take a walk out and get some fresh air?" Joan smiled. That would do her some good. So she hurried and finished, then took care of the brushes and pail. Outside, the wind stirred with a warm breeze, and she stretched and sighed. Taking deep breaths, she began to walk toward the wharf.

The wharf was empty, and she sat down with her legs dangling over the water. Her gaze traveled out over the water. England was somewhere far across that endless line of blue. She did not miss it and did not feel sorry for its trouble with America. Why should they suddenly want to tax them when they left them alone for so long? She lifted her face into the wind that stirred the few loose strands of hair. She heard a soft footstep; a girl about her own age came slowly down the wharf toward her. Joan waited. At last, the girl stood beside her. "May I sit down?" she asked. Joan nodded. The girl sat down, then after a moment of silence, she said, "My name is Molly Deeks."

Joan smiled then said softly, "My name is Joan."

The girl smiled. "Joan what?" Joan just shrugged and held out her hands in front of her. Molly smiled. "Never mind." She looked off across the ocean. "Where do you come from?" she asked.

"England," Joan said.

"Oh, I've always wanted to go to England. I come from Barbados," Molly said. Joan looked at her in surprise. "It was the most beautiful place on earth. I bet you miss England." Joan just shrugged. Molly took it as a yes and said, "I really miss Barbados. It was nothing like this place."

"Joan, hey. Joan!" Jamerson came running down the wharf, his red hair flying in the breeze. Joan leaped to her feet. "Joan, come home quick. Kurt and I got you a present!" Then he grabbed her by the hand and ran back toward the Hoods' house.

In the kitchen, Kurt stood holding a basket, and Martha stood nearby, beaming. "Come on," Jamerson said. Kurt held out the basket to her. Joan took it slowly and lifted back the napkin over the top. Then her eyes grew large with wonder and delight. Inside lay a tiny tan puppy.

"Oh, he's so cute!" breathed Joan, picking him out of the basket. Kurt and Jamerson grinned. "He's so tiny!" Joan said.

Kurt laughed. "He won't be for long. See them feet? He's a mastiff, and before you can blink, he'll be up to your waist." Joan stared at the tiny wriggling puppy in her hands. That was hard to believe.

Chapter 6

Joan knelt at the hearth, drawing out a loaf of golden white bread. Suddenly, the front door banged, and Kurt's and Jamerson's angry voices came clearly. "Two-faced coward!" Kurt said angrily, and she heard the stamp of his boot as he knocked the dust off it.

"What are they going to do about it?" Jamerson asked. Joan straightened and placed the bread on the table, still listening.

"I don't know, but whatever they do, I want to help!" Kurt said.

"Me too," Jamerson said, and the two stamped into the kitchen. Joan cut off a piece of bread for each of them and spread it thickly with butter. The boys continued their conversation. "I don't see how he could do such a thing!" Jamerson said.

"I wish Father was here. If he was, he'd show that two-faced tax collector what for!" Kurt said.

Jamerson laughed. "Make him walk the plank for a whole voyage."

Kurt shook his head. "Naw, take him out and feed him to the sharks."

"Sharks are too good for the likes of him!" Jamerson said angrily.

Joan watched the rising anger in the two boys. She was dying of curiosity. What were they so worked up about? But she held her tongue, knowing sometime or another she would find out.

At the evening meal, Kurt and Jamerson had still not given up on their talk. Martha listened to it for several minutes, then her fist came down on the table hard. "That's enough!" she cried, her gray eyes flashing with anger at the two boys. "I will hear no more of such talk!"

Kurt and Jamerson looked out of the corner of their eyes at each other. "We didn't mean nothing by it," Kurt said apologetically. "It's just that Mr. Dell seemed like such a decent fellow until he started collecting taxes!" Now Joan understood. A month before, a rich and prosperous man and his wife and son had moved into the town. Perplexed at the amount of money he seemed to have, the townspeople had held aloof from him for the first week or so until he proved to be a good friend. So now, it seemed like he had moved in to collect taxes. Even as she realized what the problem was, she heard the voices of an angry mob. Then there was the pounding on the front door.

Kurt jumped to his feet and hurried to the door before his mother could stop him. "What's going on here?" she heard him yell.

"Come with us. We're going to scare that no-good tax collector out!"

"I'm coming!" Kurt yelled over the roar.

Jamerson jumped from the table and ran to the entry before Joan could stop him. Within a second, the two boys were gone. Martha sighed and put her head in her hand. "Now what are they going to do?" Joan stood up and went to the door, peeking out into the street. The mob moved on, stopping at other houses.

An hour later, Jamerson and Kurt came tripping into the house, shouting with laughter. Jamerson held his sides with both arms. "What is going on?" Martha asked the two boys.

"Ma, you'll never guess what we did!" Kurt said.

Martha frowned at him. "What did you do?" she asked.

"We all went down to Mr. Dell's house. We told him if he wasn't out of town in half an hour, then we would tar and feather him." Martha gasped. "Aw, Ma, it didn't come to that!" said Kurt. "He and his family could only take what they could carry on their backs." Martha frowned slightly.

"And a carriage," Jamerson put in.

"We helped them along by hitching up their horses for them while they packed some bags," Kurt continued. "But you should have seen their faces, Ma." And he chuckled.

"Scared as can be!" Jamerson said.

Martha wasn't a bit amused. "I completely disagree with the collector, but I will not have you two mixed up with a mob!" she said. "Do you understand me?" Kurt and Jamerson nodded solemnly, well, as solemnly as they could. "Now it's time for bed. Get right up there," Martha spluttered. Joan stood in the corner, a very small smile touching her lips; she, for one, wished she could have seen the face of Mr. Dell.

Joan knelt in the garden, pulling the weeds. "Hello." She looked up at the strange yet almost familiar voice. Molly Deeks was at the fence surrounding the garden. She smiled and nodded. Molly leaned on the fence. "Want to go pick flowers with me?" Joan smiled and nodded, pulling out the last weed. Then she straightened and hurried into the house.

Martha was sewing a torn curtain. "Ma'am?" Joan said quietly.

Martha looked up. "One of the girls from town just asked me if I wanted to go pick flowers with her. May I go?" Martha beamed and nodded, glad that Joan had finally made a friend. Joan hurried out to where Molly was waiting. The two girls struck off toward the nearby woods.

As they walked through the knee-deep grass, they picked the wildflowers growing there. "I love flowers," said Molly. "These are definitely not as pretty as the ones back home, but when I smell them, it's almost like I have a piece of home with me."

Joan smiled. She loved the flowers. In England, she had never even touched a flower. Now she wanted to smell each one and to look closely at it. The girls wandered further and further away from the town. Soon they had entered the woods, going deeper and deeper, yet keeping track of where they went. Soon their hands were completely full of flowers, and they just wandered around. Molly talked mostly, telling Joan of Barbados. "It is strange," Molly said, "because you have eyes just the color of the sea in the harbors there."

Joan smiled. "Really?" Molly nodded.

Suddenly, the two girls heard the clatter of horses' hooves and the *tap, tap, tap* of feet. Joan lay a finger across her lips, and the two girls crept forward, peeking around trees and bushes. Then they saw them: a long line of British regulars. "Captain, what if they have the arms hidden before we get there?" Joan heard a man on horseback ask.

"They won't. We'll get in there and get their arms and be out before they can know what's happening. We've been careful so as not to let any information out," said the captain.

Joan looked at Molly. She was watching the soldiers without a bit of alarm. Joan turned and began to hurry away from the spot. Molly followed. Then when they were out of earshot from the soldiers, Joan said, "We have to go warn the townsfolk to hide the arms."

"Why?" Molly asked. "Because the soldiers will confiscate them!" Joan said, and then streaked off toward town, as the crow flew. She knew only if she was lucky could she get there in time and warn the people. Maybe if they were lucky, they could move the arms. Molly followed. From years of running the London streets, she now flew along. Molly could hardly keep her in sight.

Joan ducked and dodged trees. Then she broke out on the hill over the town. Who would act fastest? She thought to herself. The boys. She knew it was against the rules, but she ran right down the street to the meeting house where school was held. She flung the door open. Twenty pairs of shocked eyes turned toward her. "Joan!" Kurt and Jamerson were on their feet.

"Quick!" Joan gasped. "Soldiers!"

Kurt rushed forward. "Soldiers? What?" Joan took a deep breath.

"Confiscate…arms…" Then she began again. "Redcoat soldiers are coming. They're going to confiscate the firearms this town holds!"

Kurt nodded, knowing full well that she was speaking the truth. "Come on, boys!" Before the schoolmaster could stop them, the boys had rushed from the meetinghouse, calling, "Get carts and wagons!"

Within a minute, several carts were lined up before the only brick building in town, and men and boys were loading gunpowder, firearms, lead, and the one cannon the town owned onto the carts. Kurt knew of a secret place where they could store everything while the Redcoats looked for the firearms. Then the keeper of the building locked it back up, and the ones who had been guarding it took their places, and everyone went about their business. Several men dragged branches with the leaves over the tracks made by the carts and then threw away the branches.

Just after, they heard the *rat-tat-tat, rat-tat-tat* of the British drums. The British came down the street, looking proud of themselves. The townspeople watched with curiosity as they stopped before the building. The captain said something sharp to the guard, and he handed him the keys to the door. The captain opened the door and then said to his men in a loud voice, "There you go, fellows. Confiscate everything inside!"

The men tramped inside, and a moment later, a corporal came out. "Sir," he said, saluting smartly. "There is nothing in there!" The captain, who had been standing aside, smiling slyly, stared at him in disbelief for a moment, then shoved past him into the empty building.

Joan, who stood across the street watching, heard him, even though she was across the street, cussing up a storm. "Rebels!" he shouted after a moment of saying unrepeatable words. "We'll level this whole town someday!" Then he stormed out of the building, his soldiers following. From the street corners and windows of buildings, the people's jeers followed them out of town. When they had disappeared from sight in the trees, Joan noticed Molly standing at the edge of the road.

As the soldiers passed, she dropped them a low curtsy. Joan's jaw dropped. Why did Molly do that? She walked forward, and Molly turned toward her. "Where have you been?" Molly asked. Her face was damp, and her eyes bulging a bit.

"I told you I came to warn the people to hide their arms!" Joan said.

"Why?" Molly asked, her brow furrowing into a frown.

"Because I told you that too. The soldiers would confiscate them!"

"Molly!" someone called before Molly could answer. Molly turned. "Coming, Aunt Rosy!" she called and hurried toward the woman who was calling her name.

Joan then headed toward home. "What's been going on?" Martha asked when Joan came in.

"Soldiers came to confiscate the town's firearms," Joan explained.

Martha's face paled. "They didn't get them, did they?" Joan shook her head.

"Kurt and Jamerson have more details," she said and washed her hands.

"Where are the flowers you went to pick?" Martha asked.

Joan blushed slightly. "I lost them in the excitement." Martha smiled and nodded.

Right then, the door banged open. "Mother!" It was Kurt. "The *Martha* is coming into harbor!"

Martha jumped to her feet. "Come on, Joan," she cried, reaching for her shawl.

Joan stood back. The *Martha* was Captain Hood's ship, named after Martha. "What if I stay here and clean up a bit and get dinner going so there will be something to eat when he comes back?" she asked.

Martha looked up at her. "Very well, dear. See you later!" Then she was out the door, letting it shut softly behind her. Joan went to the fire, stirred up the coals, and set to work.

Chapter 7

Two hours later, Joan heard the front door bang and then the all-too-well-remembered voice of Captain Hood mingled with that of Martha, Kurt, and Jamerson. Joan had set the table, and the dinner was ready, so she set it out. "Well now, Joan," Captain Hood's voice boomed, making her jump. "I see you've grown."

Joan looked up shyly. "Thank you, sir," she smiled slightly.

"It looks like dinner is ready. We had better sit down and eat. James, you'll see how good of a cook Joan has become."

"She had better be a good cook." The captain smiled. "Because I'm a hungry man."

*****

Joan lay back into the pillows in her bed, staring up at the ceiling. Was it truly only four months since she had come to the Hoods'? There was a knock on the door. "Come in," she called.

The door opened a crack, and Jamerson poked his head in. "You awake?" he asked.

Joan nodded and smiled. "Come in." Jamerson came in and sat down on a chair near the bed.

"You were awfully quiet at dinner," he said. "Is something wrong?"

Joan looked up in surprise. "No, why?" she asked.

"Just because you're much quieter than usual. Captain was wondering if he offended you."

Joan looked up in surprise. "Of course, not! He's a kind and decent gentleman! He didn't offend me."

Jamerson smiled. "He'll be glad to hear that. But why were you so quiet?"

"I just can't find it easy to face strangers."

"Captain isn't a stranger."

"I know, but he's been gone for four months, and in that time, we've become strangers."

Jamerson frowned slightly. "Why are you so wary of strangers?" he asked.

Joan looked up at him quietly. How could she tell him of the hundreds of times she had had to steer clear of strangers to keep them together? Of the many friendships she had dodged to make sure nobody would turn on them and give away their hiding places? No, she couldn't tell him. She shrugged. "I guess I'm just not the friendly type."

Jamerson frowned again. "You are too. I know you, and you are friendly, but you're tighter than a clam with strangers." Joan just shrugged since she had no answer. "You haven't even opened up to Martha and Kurt, and we've lived with them for four months," Jamerson said. She could tell that this matter had been weighing heavily on his mind. "Do you realize today was the first time you've spoken to Kurt without him speaking to you first?"

Joan looked up in surprise. "He spoke to me first," she said. Jamerson thought, then nodded.

"Yes," he said dryly. "I guess he did." Joan waited. "I really wish you would open up a bit to them." Joan smiled, knowing that as much as she might want to, that would be one of the few things she couldn't do for him. Jamerson waited and then shrugged. "Well then, good night. See you in the morning." Joan nodded, and he went out.

The next morning, Joan was up early and was stirring up the coals in the fireplace when Captain Hood came into the kitchen. "Good morning, Joan," he said.

Joan looked up. "Good morning, sir," she said shyly.

"I brought something for you. You were so busy last night I didn't have a chance to give it to you."

He held out toward her a package. Joan stood up and took the package. It was something hard. She opened it. Inside lay a small leather-bound book. Joan lifted the book in her hands. On the front was burned the words *Elanor May Rindle*. Joan looked up at the captain with a smile. "Thank you." He nodded, a secret smile dancing in his eyes. Joan laid the book carefully on the table.

It wasn't until that afternoon that Joan got her first glimpses into the new book. It was a diary, and the first page read:

May 3, 1758

Dear Dairy,

My name is Elanor Mary. I keep this journal as I become a mother. Yesterday I had a beautiful baby girl. She has the most hair of any child I've seen, and I've seen many children considering that I am a midwife. John said we should name her Elanor after me, but I think we should name her Joan because I love that name.

Joan stopped. *Joan*, this woman had picked the very name that Joan herself had. She continued.

If I do get to name her Joan, I shall name her Joan Anna. It's a strange name, but Joan was the name of my mother, and Anna is the name of John's. I believe she will look like myself. But like all babies, it will take a few weeks to determine.

June 2, 1758

Dear Dairy,

We have named our little girl Joan Anna. She is so beautiful. I think that she will look like me, and so does John. I think he was hoping for a boy to be the first child, but he loves Joan so much. She's the most happy child I've ever seen. She has John's eyes, though—a deep, beautiful turquoise fringed with the longest black lashes I have ever seen. She has blond hair like me. I can hardly wait to see whether or not it will stay blond. But she is growing so fast, it's unbelievable!

Joan frowned slightly. She had turquoise eyes and blond hair; her name was Joan. This book, whose was it? She continued to read.

January 1, 1759

Dear Dairy,

Can you believe it? My daughter's first New Year! She does have blond hair; I can't believe how beautiful she is. I have never seen such a happy baby! John is so proud of her. He says she has his fighting spirit, which I believe. Though I've never seen little Joan get angry, she is brave too. John took her onto the London Bridge and held her over the side. Heaven knows how frightened I was! But Joan wasn't; she seemed to like it, glowing and cooing. She is a strong little baby, already standing and taking her first steps. In fact, I've never seen a child so strong! It's so bittersweet to see how fast she grows and takes her first steps! John and I may not have everything, but we've got little Joan, and we could ask for nothing more!

May 2, 1759

Dear Dairy,

My little daughter's first birthday! Oh, it was such a happy day. John made her a little dollhouse, and I made her a dolly out of old rags. Joan was so delighted and hugged the dolly, saying over and over,

"Tank uo, tank uo." She's so mannerly and loves to be near me in whatever I do. John was so proud of it being her first birthday, so he took her out on a walk and told every person that stopped to compliment him on how beautiful his daughter was, that it was her first birthday. The people were so delighted, and many gave her little treats. A baker gave John a whole cake! I couldn't believe it, and an apple woman gave him a whole pound of apples. A jeweler gave John a beautiful brooch! He gave it to me, saying it would be an heirloom and that when Joan was older, she would have it.

Joan smiled. This woman was mighty proud of her daughter. She smiled wistfully thinking of all the fun the mother and daughter must be having at that very moment. She continued to read.

June 4, 1760

Dear Dairy,

I am expecting my second child! How I pray it shall be a boy! Joan is so happy that she will be a big sister and keeps asking when the baby will come. When John gets home from work, she runs over to him, crying, "Papa!" Then when he picks her up, she'll ask, "Baby?" in her childish way. "Not yet," John will say, smiling. "Not yet. Just wait." Joan watches me sewing the tiny garments that once were hers into new ones and says, "Baby? Those for baby?" I'll smile and say, "Yes, Joan. These are for the baby." Then she takes each folded garment and stacks it neatly in the cradle and says, "There now, Baby won't have a messy room." She's so happy over this new baby. Once, I asked her what she thought it should be. She sat there for a moment, then said, "Boy, Papa, want boy." Every day she gets more excited about the coming baby. It is due any day now.

June 6, 1760

Dear Dairy,

It is a boy! I can't believe it! He's so beautiful, and Joan is over the moon! She insists on seeing him every time he is awake. Then she pats his head softly and says in a whisper, "Sleep, sleep, baby." She is so happy and is always quiet so that "baby can sleep."
John and I have named him Jamerson.

Joan jumped to her feet, her eyes wide as she stared at the book she held. "Joan!" Joan looked up. Jamerson and Kurt were walking down the street toward her. Joan jumped off the porch. "Jamerson!" she cried, running toward him. "Look!" She held up the book. "It's our mother's diary. Our last name is…" She peered at the front of the book. "Rindle!"

Jamerson stared at her. "What are you talking about?" he asked.

"Look!" Joan cried, holding out the book. "It says right there, our mother's name!" Jamerson walked forward and took the book. Still standing in the street, he read the pages Joan had. He looked up at her in complete surprise.

"It describes your looks to perfection!" he said.

Joan laughed softly, her whole face shining. "I never even dared to hope I would find out my name!" Joan said.

Jamerson grinned. "Let's keep reading it." Kurt grinned and walked past them into the house, and Joan and Jamerson sat down on the steps while Joan continued to read out loud.

…He's such a fine baby. Just like Joan
he's quiet and doesn't cry much.

September 28, 1760

Dear Diary,
  Jamerson and Joan are so happy together and Jamerson looks just like John did when he was a baby. He has bright red hair and blue eyes. My eyes are blue so he has my eyes like Joan has John's.

Together they read on reading of special events in their lives. Then they reached a page that read in shaky handwriting.

August 6, 1765

  This is John Rindle writing because I believe there should be an end to this here diary. Elanor died last night because of unknown sickness. There was nothing the doctor could do. Joan and Jamerson don't understand what has happened to their mother.

There was no more writing. Joan stared blankly at the book in her hands. "Where did you get this?" Jamerson asked. Joan looked up.

"The captain gave it to me." Jamerson frowned slightly.

"Where did he get it?"

"I don't know. Let's go ask him." Jamerson nodded, and the two headed toward the wharf where Captain Hood was putting a few repairs onto the Martha. He looked up when Joan and Jamerson approached him.

"Well now, isn't this a surprise!" he said, smiling.

The two were silent for a moment, and then Jamerson held up the diary. "Captain sir, where did you get this?" he asked. The captain reached out and took the book.

"When I got back to England," he began, "I started looking around for your folks, but I really couldn't find anything. Then one day, this little old lady comes to me and says, 'I hear you're looking for a man and woman that were parents to two children. A girl about fourteen and a boy about twelve.' Well, I say, 'Yes, I am, what's the concern of it to you?' Then she says, 'This girl, does she have blond hair and turquoise eyes?' 'Yes,' I say to her, and she smiles. 'The boy, does he have red hair and blue eyes? The strangest red hair you've ever seen?' Again, I tell her that she is right. Then she gives me this here book along with a few other things and says, 'You give these things to them children because they'll want them.' Then she left, and I never even got her name."

Joan and Jamerson looked at each other. "What is this book?" Captain Hood asked.

"Our mother's diary," Jamerson said.

Captain Hood smiled. "Do you want the other things she gave to me to give to you?"

Jamerson and Joan nodded. "Yes, sir," Jamerson said.

Captain Hood turned and called to Jerry, who was working on the deck. "Jerry, can you get that bundle out of my cabin?" Jerry nodded and disappeared below deck. A few minutes later, he returned, carrying a bundle about the size of two large watermelons. He brought it to Captain Hood. The captain gave it to the two waiting children without a word.

Chapter 8

Joan and Jamerson knelt before the bundle in Joan's room. Joan pulled back the heavy quilt that was tied around the bundle. As the quilt fell back, they saw a small box, a large leather-bound Bible, a bigger box about a foot long, a foot deep, and a foot wide, and a small velvet bag. Joan reached out and picked up the small box. It was only about an inch tall, about four inches long, and about three inches wide. On the top was a carved leaves and acorns. There was a small catch, and Joan pressed it. The lid of the box flipped open, and a very soft melody floated out from a small space of a tiny turning cylinder with small teeth.

On the other side was a tiny bag. Joan lifted it out, and Jamerson leaned forward. Joan opened it and looked inside. She gasped softly and lifted out a small delicate silver ring. "This must have been our mother's," Joan said, holding it in her palm.

"I guess so," Jamerson said. Joan put the ring back into the bag and laid the bag back into the music box. Jamerson picked up the velvet bag and opened it. "Look!" he breathed and lifted out a gold watch.

Joan gasped. "It's beautiful!" she cried.

Jamerson popped the lid. "Look," he said, turning it toward her. "What does that say?"

Joan took the watch and read, "To John Havre Rindle from James George Dex." She looked up at Jamerson. "This was our father's." She held it out to him. "It is yours now." Jamerson took the watch carefully. He wound it, then held it to his ear. The soft tick, tick, filled the silent room. Then Joan reached out and pulled the large box toward her. Inside were two small books and a scroll. Joan reached in and picked up the scroll. She unrolled it. On it were painted faces with names on it. "It's a family tree!" she cried. "Look!" She pointed to the bottom where two faces were painted. Beneath the face of a pretty woman with blond hair and blue eyes was written the name Elanor Mary Rindle. Under the face of a red-haired man with turquoise eyes was the name John Havre Rindle. "It's like her diary says. You do look like our father," Joan said to Jamerson.

Jamerson smiled and peered closer at the faces. "And you look like our mother." Joan blushed slightly. If she really did look like her mother, she must be pretty. "Let's look at the Bible," Jamerson said, lifting the heavy Bible. On a blank page at the front were written the names.

John Havre Rindle born January 6, 1739. Died
October 17, 1765. Married to Elanor Mary Vess. Born
September 10, 1741. Died August 5, 1765

Beneath the names was written:

Children.
Joan Anna Rindle. Born May 2, 1758.
Jamerson Blake Rindle. Born June 6, 1760

Joan ran a hand over the page and then looked up at Jamerson. "It's your job to keep the Bible now. You'll have to write our marriages and our children. In time, perhaps my death." Jamerson nodded solemnly and took the Bible.

Joan knew her name and her heritage. She now knew where she came from because one of the little books in the large box had been her father's journal. From it, she had found out that he had been eighteen when he had married her mother. Her mother had been sixteen. Elanor Mary Rindle had been a midwife since she was fifteen and a midwife helper since she was twelve. Both she and John Havre Rindle were born in Switzerland. After they were married, they moved to England, where Joan and Jamerson were born. The one who gave the watch, they found out, was John Rindle's best friend; it was a wedding gift. The music box was also a wedding gift from Elanor's mother.

*****

Joan was quieter than ever before because of the many thoughts that filled her head. Captain Hood left for distant trading shores, and August turned into September, and Joan faced her first autumn in America.

Joan sat at the table peeling potatoes when she heard Kurt and Jamerson coming into the entry, talking in worried tones. "Five hundred pounds is a fortune!" she heard Jamerson say.

"No one would arrest John Brown and his fellows for five hundred pounds!" Kurt scoffed.

"Oh yes, they would!" Jamerson said. "That is a lot of money." The two boys went upstairs, and their talk was lost.

Five hundred pounds for the capture of John Brown and his men! That was a lot of money, and as Jamerson had said, many people would try to win it. John Brown and his fellows had better look out!

She finished peeling the potatoes and was cutting them when she heard a knock on the door. Martha was gone for the afternoon. Molly stood at the door. "Hello." She smiled when Joan opened the door.

Joan smiled. "Won't you come in?" she asked. Molly nodded and followed her into the kitchen. Joan set out a plate of cookies and a cup of milk. "I must continue with my work," she said and began cutting the potatoes again.

"I wanted to ask you," Molly said, reaching for a cookie. "Why did you not want the soldiers to confiscate the town's arms?"

Joan looked up in surprise. "Because they had no right. Those arms are for the town. The town made and deserved them."

Molly frowned slightly. "But everything here belongs to the king." Joan's knife stopped, and she looked at Molly in surprise.

"Do you really believe that?" she asked.

Molly shrugged. "Why not?"

Joan frowned. "These people worked hard. The king abandoned them for years! Then one day when things look prosperous, he thinks, *Oh well, now I get everything those poor wretches in America own!* Well, those poor wretches in America won't stand for it, and they shouldn't. The king sits there on his throne and doesn't lift his hand to a bit of work! He has never known what true hunger is like. He suddenly sees the prospect of wealth unlike anything he would find in England and wants it. Well, he can't have it. The Americans will stand up and put their foot down. They'll stand tall and won't break under the greedy king." Her chin went up in a proud gesture. "Lord knows how I wish I was one of them!"

Molly frowned. "How can an Englander like you believe such things?" she asked.

Joan's eyes flashed. "Because I've been there! I've seen England. I've seen hunger. I've seen times when I had only one ragged dress to wear day after day for months! I've seen work like the King himself would never imagine doing! Up at 5:00 a.m. and working until midnight just to keep a roof over my head and my brother fed! I've seen the convents filled with orphaned children whose parents have been killed or have died. Those convents are like ice. They haven't a care about the children, just so long as they're off the streets. They don't mind breaking up families! If America is a place where I can live free and my brother can have what he wishes, where I can stand up tall and proud for what I believe in, then why not fight for it? People ask, what if it causes war? Well, bring on the war, I say. I've seen the English Army. It's trained and drilled. But one thing it hasn't got that Americans have is spirit and pride! Americans won't give up. They'll fight, and believe me, it won't be easy, but they'll win!" She stopped. It was the most she had ever remembered talking.

"I'm glad you feel that way." She looked up quickly. Kurt stood in the doorway, grinning. Joan went quickly back to work. Kurt came over and sat down at the table and picked up a cookie. "You see, Molly, why us Americans want to be free?" he asked.

Molly nodded slowly. "I guess so." She looked up at Joan. "You've never told anyone much about your life in England."

Joan scooped the potatoes into a bowl. "I've said too much already." She went to the fireplace, dumped them into a pot of boiling water, and then drew out a loaf of cornbread from the ashes.

*****

As each month passed, autumn turned into winter. Just before the harbor froze, the Martha came sailing into the harbor and was docked there for the winter. Captain Hood would work in town through the winter, and when spring came, he'd repair his ship and set it back out to sea. Winter came with such snowstorms that Joan was often afraid. But she didn't mention it. She still didn't talk much and was quiet. In the Hoods' household, there was no Christmas since they didn't believe in it. Joan and Jamerson had never really celebrated it either. Then the new year dawned with bright new promises.

Joan looked out the window at the softly falling flakes. It was hard to believe she had been at the Hoods' for only nine months.

Her hair now hung to her waist in a shiny mass of golden curls. She was close now to being fifteen, in a few more months. She heard the front door bang and then the boys' voices. They had been out sledding. They came in, shrugging out of their heavy coats. Joan had warmed some milk, and she now gave them some with cornbread spread with maple sugar frosting. The two boys ate, talking about the day. Jamerson looked up at her. "You should have seen Rudy Winn! He can't sled anymore!" At the question in Joan's eyes, he chuckled.

"Too big. That one's a giant. He's just fifteen, but he's already six feet two!" Kurt said, grinning.

"He could sled just fine last year, but this year…" He shook his head. "Grown like a weed. But he can give you a push-off that'll send you clear out onto the lake. Strong as a bull too." Jamerson laughed. "Tried going down the slop and busted his sled right in half. Should have seen his face!" The two boys laughed. "But he's a good sport. Spent all morning giving the rest of us push-offs."

"Then there was little Tommy Dell. He's about as small as Rudy is big." Jamerson smirked. "My size and he's nearly fifteen." Kurt about choked on his cornbread. This sent Jamerson into a howl of laughter. Kurt coughed and then sputtered, "I remember last year he ran into a snowbank and disappeared completely! We literally had to dig away the snowbank before we found him."

Jamerson snickered. "Today he went out on the ice and almost hit the black ice. You should have seen the moves he was making trying to steer his sled away from it." The two boys guffawed loudly. Joan watched them with an unamused air. She couldn't see what was so funny.

Martha came into the kitchen at that moment. "Boys, I just passed your room, and you left it looking like a tidal wave hit it. Run up and clean it up." The boys swallowed the last of their cornbread and left the table, still chuckling.

Joan shook her head and looked out the window. She saw Molly walking up the path toward the house and went to the door. Molly smiled when Joan opened the door. "Joan," she smiled. "My Aunt Rosy is throwing a sort of party tonight, and I was wondering if you would like to come?" Joan bit her lower lip. A whole evening with strangers sure didn't sound like a good time. Molly read her thoughts. "Of course, Jamerson and Kurt are invited too," she said. Joan sighed. "Come on, and I'll ask Martha," she said with a smile. Molly smiled and came in.

After Molly told Martha about the party, Martha called the boys. "Kurt, Jamerson. Come on down here for a moment." The boys came down, still laughing over something. "Would you two like to go to Molly's party tonight?" Martha asked.

The two boys looked at each other and shrugged. "Sure," Kurt said.

Molly beamed and turned to Joan. "Now won't you come?" Joan hesitated.

"Come on, Joan, you haven't gone to any kind of gathering besides church since we came here," Jamerson said. Joan looked at him. He grinned, and his eyes were pleading. She smiled and nodded.

Molly beamed and headed for the door. "It starts at six. Be there!" Then she hurried out into the softly falling snow.

Joan sighed. Jamerson grinned, and Martha beamed. "Joan, come here," she said, her eyes dancing, and led Joan up the stairs. She led her up into the attic. There was a large trunk in the corner. Martha went to it and opened the lid. "These are all dresses, for the most part," she said. She lifted out a cream dress. It was beautiful. She smiled. "This one is my wedding gown. Do you like it?" Joan's eyes grew large, and she nodded. Martha beamed and laid the dress carefully aside. She lifted out a black dress. Her eyes clouded slightly. "This was the dress I wore to my Eliza's burial." Joan could say nothing. Martha laid that dress away also. She lifted out several others. "These were the ones I made when I had Kurt and Eliza. James didn't want me wearing the same dress and just letting out the seams." Her eyes twinkled as she laid the dresses aside. "He always brought me new fabric so that I could make some new dresses." She leaned back toward the trunk. Her face sobered, and her eyes clouded. She lifted out a white baby dress. "This was Eliza's christening dress," she said softly. Joan took a half-halting step forward. She started to lift a hand then dropped it and said nothing. Martha laid the dress aside. Then she smiled and lifted out an oil painting the size of her palm. She held it out toward Joan. "That's her." Joan took the picture. From the painting looked back a small round face fringed with black curls. Gray eyes stared back from the paint. "Her skin was a bit more honey-colored than it is in the painting," Martha said.

Joan smiled. "She was a beautiful child." Martha smiled and took the painting.

"She was, wasn't she?" She laid aside the painting, then her eyes lighted, and she reached into the trunk and lifted out a soft blue dress. "Here!" She smiled. "I was about your age when I went to my first party. It will match your complexion. Here" She held it out toward Joan.

"It's yours now." Joan stared at her in disbelief. "But…" she stammered.

"It's yours. It should go to a daughter." Martha smiled slightly. "My daughter is dead. You're my best excuse now. If you don't have it, then it will just get old, and I'll have to throw it away."

Joan smiled. "Thank you," she said and took the dress.

Chapter 9

Joan put on the dress and looked down at it. It was beautiful. She had combed her hair up, and soft curls had escaped the comb and fringed her face. As hard as she tried, she couldn't get them in place. So she left them and put on her slippers. There, now she was ready to leave. "Joan!" Jamerson hollered right then. "Are you coming?" Joan went quickly out of the room and down the stairs. "About time!" Jamerson said. "Girls spend so much time fussing over themselves." Joan smiled but said nothing. "Come on," Jamerson said. "It's almost six!"

Captain Hood stood at the door. He smiled as he handed Joan her shawl. "You look right pretty, Joan," he said. Joan beamed, her eyes lighting. She had come to show more feeling toward the captain since he was the one who delivered to her, her name and heritage. She flipped the shawl about her shoulders and set out with the boys.

"I can't wait to let you meet my new friends," Jamerson told her. "You'll like them." Joan raised an eyebrow as though to ask how he knew she would like them. "Because they're so much like me and Kurt. And I'm your brother, and Kurt, well, he's sort of my brother, so you see? You'll like them."

Joan smiled. Perhaps. But at the door, Molly grabbed her by the arm and said, "Come on, Joan. I'd like you to meet my friends." Joan hesitated and looked at Jamerson.

"Go ahead," Jamerson grinned. "I'll talk to you later." Then he headed toward a group of boys nearby. Joan followed Molly hesitantly toward a large group of girls.

"Girls!" Molly quieted their chatter. "I'd like you to meet Joan Anna Rindle." The girls seemed surprised that she had a three-word name.

A tall one stepped forward. "I've been dying to meet you, but you always keep yourself hidden away." She smiled, tossing back a black curl, and shook Joan's hand. Joan smiled, then looked down. "My, aren't you a shy one!" the girl said. "My name is Linda Pel."

Joan looked up again and flickered a smile then said softly, "I'm glad to meet you."

Linda squealed in delight. "Oh, Joan, I just adore your accent!"

Joan blushed and looked down again. Another girl stepped forward. She looked somewhat like the first, only shorter. "My name is Daisy Pel. I'm Linda's sister. I'm very glad to meet you." Joan nodded and flashed her a shy smile before looking back down.

One by one, the girls introduced themselves, and then Molly's aunt called, "Alright, children. Quiet!" The talk stopped, and everyone turned toward her. "Now you all know how to dance, so we'll start the dancing off with the French minuet." Molly's aunt smiled at them all.

During the winter, Martha had taught Joan to dance, and she had taken to it like a duck to water. Joan shrank back into the shadows as a group of boys near the group of girls. Molly and several others were chosen; Joan sighed softly. That was over with.

"May I have this dance?" Joan jumped and turned quickly around. Kurt stood grinning. "Sorry if I spooked you," he said.

Joan sighed. "No, it's fine. I mean, yes…" She stammered, reddening with embarrassment. "Yes, you may have this dance," she said after a moment. Kurt smiled and led her to the dance floor. Joan saw Jamerson dancing also. He was good at dancing. "So how do you like Molly's party so far?" Kurt asked her as the music started, and they took their places. She stood opposite him, then they came forward, and she curtsied, and he bowed. The dance seemed awfully boring to Joan, but she said nothing and danced beautifully. Kurt kept the conversation going. Perhaps it was because he expected little or any answers that they had fun, even though it was boring. He talked as though he didn't want an answer, only asking very few questions.

Joan had to admit that for a regular girl, the dance might have been the most delightful event that had happened all year, but to Joan, it was just short of torture. Half the boys she danced with asked way too many questions. About the middle of the party, Jamerson came over and said, "Come on, I'd like you to meet my friends now." So Joan followed him to a group of about six boys. Kurt was among them. Joan noticed that, in fact, most of the boys were at least two years older than Jamerson. "Fellows, I'd like you to meet my sister, Joan Anna," Jamerson said. Joan nodded, and the boys nodded back. This time, there wasn't any laughing at her accent. "This is Rudy Winn," Jamerson said, as a tall, gangly boy stepped forward. Joan suddenly remembered Kurt's and Jamerson's talk and could completely understand why he couldn't go sledding anymore. "This is Tommy Dell." The short and stocky boy stepped forward. Like Jamerson had said, he was Jamerson's size. Jamerson continued introducing his friends. Joan had to do no talking, so it was better than being introduced to Molly's. Because the boys didn't seem like they took real delight in talking either.

When Jamerson had introduced her, he led her back to Molly's friends and then left. Finally, it was time to go, and she was relieved. At the door, Molly asked, "See, Joan. Didn't you enjoy yourself?"

Joan smiled and said, "Molly, it was the best party I ever went to."

Molly beamed. She didn't know Joan had never gone to any parties at all. Then the three went home. Kurt and Jamerson talking over boy things, and Joan walking in silence.

When they reached the Hoods' house, the captain and Martha came out to the porch. "Did you enjoy yourselves?" Martha asked, and they all nodded.

Joan went straight to bed, tired and totally exhausted; she wouldn't be going to any more parties if she could help it.

The next day, Joan came out of her room. Like always, she was up before everyone else. She saw the boys' room door open, and Kurt came quietly out. He looked relieved to see her. "I think Jamerson is sick," he said quietly. Joan gasped and took a quick step to the door and pushed it open. She went to Jamerson's bed. He lay still, but his face was red and damp.

She laid a hand on his forehead. "He's burning up!" she gasped and looked up at Kurt.

"What should I do?" he asked.

"Get me some ice from the ice house. We have got to get this fever down!" Kurt hurried from the room.

Joan went to the nightstand where a basin and water sat. She dumped the water from the pitcher into the basin and grabbed the towel. She took the water to Jamerson's bed and dipped the towel in the water then wrung it out. She placed it over his forehead. He gasped, and his eyelids flickered open.

"Joan," his voice was thick. "My throat hurts!"

Joan tried to smile. "I'm sorry. I'll bring you some hot tea for it." Then she stood up and hurried from the room. Kurt was in the kitchen breaking up a large cube of ice into a basin. Joan smiled and nodded then went to the fire and stirred it up. She put on a kettle of water.

As the day continued, Jamerson only got worse. His fever increased despite the ice and cold rags Joan packed around him. By that night, he was unconscious. He chilled and fevered in turn. Joan sat with him all day. Martha tried to help, but everything she tried to do, Joan had already done. Throughout the night, Joan sat with him, packing cold towels on him when he was fevering and putting the blankets on him when he chilled. Morning came, and he was still worse. He was having trouble breathing. The sound of his troubled breathing filled the whole room. Joan sat with him, not having breakfast. Kurt went off to school alone. Captain Hood had nothing to do but leave for his job also. Martha busied herself around the house, and Joan fussed over Jamerson.

Slowly evening approached, and Jamerson was still worse. Joan ate a small amount of dinner. "Get some rest, Joan," Martha told her gently. "You can't care for him if you're sick yourself."

"Maybe in the morning," Joan mumbled, watching Jamerson's hot face.

"Very well," Martha sighed. Kurt was sleeping on some blankets in front of the fire downstairs. Joan sat by the bed, but through the night, there was no change, but Jamerson didn't get worse.

In the morning, Joan asked Captain Hood to ask the doctor to come by on his way to work. A few minutes after the captain left, the doctor arrived. Joan showed him to Jamerson's room. "I'll let some blood and see what that does," the doctor said. He let the blood and then said to Joan, "Now don't you worry. Keep trying to get the warm tea down him and perhaps some gruel." Joan nodded, and he laid a hand on her shoulder just for a moment, then left. Joan did as the doctor said, but still, Jamerson didn't get better.

That night, the doctor came again and let more blood and left. When he had left, Martha came in. "Joan dear, don't you think you should get some rest? You didn't have any this morning. You're surely going to get sick." Joan shook her head. Martha sighed and left the room.

Joan sat by the bed, watching the light from the candle dance across Jamerson's face. She looked around. On the shelf on the nightstand on Jamerson's side was their Bible. She lifted it and opened it. She tried reading it but could not concentrate. She closed it and put it back on the shelf. She looked back toward Jamerson. He lay still, the sound of his breathing filling the room. A soft sob caught in her throat. She couldn't lose him. She sighed softly and stood up and went to the window. The night sky was clear and full of millions of stars. She stood there for a moment. Then she began to pray;

it sounded more like a conversation than a prayer though. "He's awful sick, God, and I don't know what to do. I've tried everything and nothing seems to work. Couldn't you heal him like you healed all them others in the Bible? I just can't lose him. He's everything I've got, everything I've ever lived for." She felt tears in her eyes for the first time. She looked toward the bed, and to her complete and almost terror, Jamerson's eyes were open, and he was watching her.

"Joan?" he said, and his voice was weak.

With a soft sob, she almost ran to his side. "Jamerson!" she cried and touched his forehead. Where he had been burning up a few minutes ago, there was no fever. "How do you feel?" Joan asked him.

"A little bit hungry."

Joan nodded. "I'll grab something." Then she almost bolted toward the door, so he couldn't see the tears on her cheeks. She went down to the kitchen.

Kurt was sitting up and looked up when she came through the door. He came instantly to his feet when he saw her. "What's the matter?" he asked in worried tones.

Joan went quickly to the fire, her face turned away so that he couldn't see the tears she was so ashamed of. "Nothing," she said. "In fact, everything is going to be alright." She spooned some of the gruel Martha had made into a bowl and said, "He's awake."

It wasn't until the next day at noon that Joan got some rest. She awoke late in the day, lay there for a moment, then realized she felt strangely hot and her throat was tight. She climbed out of bed. Her whole body ached. She staggered a little, and the room spun before her eyes. She put on a dress and stood before the door while her world slowed down. She felt sick and tired. Finally, the spinning stopped, and she opened the door and went out.

"Joan dear, is that you?" Martha called and came to the bottom of the stairs. Joan nodded and went down slowly, feeling nausea sweeping up through her. "Are you alright?" Martha asked.

Joan nodded. "How's Jamerson?"

"Sleeping," Martha said, and she led her into the kitchen. Captain Hood and Kurt sat at the table. "Do you want something to eat?" Martha asked.

Joan shook her head. "Not right now." She went to the fire and sat down on the hearth, picking up the mending she hadn't done in the past couple of days. "I better catch up with the mending." Martha nodded and sat back down at the table. Joan worked while they ate. Then she helped with the dishes. By then, she was close to vomiting over her dizziness. She went up to her room and collapsed on her bed. After a few minutes, she changed and lay down.

The next morning, Joan knew she was sick; her fever was up. She staggered out of bed and got dressed. She looked in the mirror; her face was flushed, and she could tell she had a fever. She had better stay near the fire so no one would notice. She never did know how in the world she managed to get through that day. Every breath felt like a spear in her lungs, and she about burned up. Martha did not notice her sickness because Joan asked if she would entertain Jamerson while she caught up on the baking. Finally, she went up to bed. She knew she couldn't hide her sickness for much longer but was determined not to be a burden.

Joan was awake early the next morning after a sleepless night. She went down and sat next to the fire. Sitting there, head in hand, she heard a footstep in the doorway and looked up. Kurt entered the room, rubbing the sleep from his eyes. "Good morning," he said. Joan nodded mutely and reached for a bowl nearby to fill it with some corn pudding she had made. After filling it, she stood up and headed toward the table. Suddenly, the cough she had been holding back ever since Jamerson awoke came without warning, and she bent double in a fit of coughing. Kurt stood at a small mirror hanging on the wall, combing his hair. He whirled around and, in one stride, was at her side. He took the bowl from her hands, laid it on the table, and then helped her into a chair. "How long have you been sick?" he asked sharply.

Joan shook her head. "I'm not sick!" she choked. She pushed herself feebly from the chair, staggered, and fell headlong into a pool of blackness.

Chapter 10

The next few days, Joan lived in a world of half unconsciousness, half consciousness. She never knew whether it was day or night. In fact, she did not know she had been unconscious for a full two weeks! During that time, she burned with fever. She became conscious of her surroundings on the fifteenth day of her sickness. She didn't know the fever had broken, and she had been asleep until she opened her eyes. She lay there for a moment, staring at the ceiling then turned her head slowly. Martha sat by her bed. They were in the kitchen. Kurt and Jamerson sat at the table, and Jamerson had his head in his arms. Martha looked over at her when she turned her head. "Joan," she said softly. Kurt looked up and Jamerson raised his head. "How do you feel?"

Joan felt as though she were too weak to speak, but she forced one word past her cracked lips. "Fine."

"Are you hungry?" Joan shook her head ever so slightly. "Are you thirsty?" Joan nodded slightly, and Martha reached for a cup of water nearby. She lifted Joan's head so that she could swallow a few sips of water. Then Joan was so exhausted that she fell almost instantly asleep.

The next time she awoke, Captain Hood sat at her side, and there wasn't anyone else around. He gave her a drink, and then Joan forced another word past her cracked lips. "Jamerson?"

"He's fine. Going back to school now," Captain Hood assured her. Joan nodded weakly and fell once again into a deep sleep. She drifted in and out of sleep several times over the next five days. Each time she awoke, Martha or Captain Hood, whoever was sitting with her, would make her take some water and gruel. Sometimes Jamerson would be there. He didn't say much, but he looked genuinely worried. Then on the sixth day, Joan awoke and didn't feel so weak and tired. In fact, she was able to be propped up, and she brushed her own hair. She was able to remain awake for an hour or so before going back to sleep. From then, she began to gain her strength rapidly.

Over the next week, she gained strength so rapidly that she was able to sit up in her bed and take on the mending and sewing. At the end of the third week, the doctor came and said she should try taking her first steps from the bed. Joan was all too anxious. Holding onto Martha and the doctor, Joan was sat up with her legs over the edge. Then she pulled herself to her feet. That's when it struck her. She couldn't feel her left leg! She tried to move it forward, but nothing happened. So she moved her right foot forward, then tried to move her left foot. She almost fell, but the doctor caught her and helped her regain her balance. Joan tried again and again, but nothing happened. Each time she tried to move her left foot, she could not. Finally, after several tries, the doctor helped her back onto the bed. "Keep trying," he said. "You're still weak."

Joan tried. Oh, how she tried. She worked hard and tried hard, but neither seemed to help much. Martha would watch with cloudy eyes as Joan tried again and again, wincing when she would fall and hurrying to help her up. Jamerson helped her. They worked for a week before Jamerson lost patience. "Can't you just walk?" he exploded after Joan almost fell for the tenth time that day.

"I'm trying," Joan said quietly.

"If you were trying, you'd be walking by now!" Jamerson said and stormed out of the room. Joan watched him go, then collapsed on the bed. What was the matter with her leg? Why wouldn't it help her move and walk? That night, after everyone had gone to bed, she practiced again, taking several tumbles in the meantime. She had just dragged herself back up to a sitting position when she heard footsteps on the stairs. Trying as hard as she could, she managed to drag herself up onto the bed.

Kurt entered the kitchen. "What do you think you're doing?" he asked. Joan pretended to be asleep. "You can't fool me. What are you doing?" Joan opened one eye and looked at him. "Nothing."

"Practicing walking?" Kurt asked. Joan didn't say anything. He walked over to the table and sat down. "What's wrong, Joan?" he asked.

"Huh?" Joan asked. "What's wrong? Why aren't you walking by now?"

Joan shrugged. "I just need to practice more," she said, rising on her elbow.

"Practice!" Kurt snorted. "You've been practicing every day for the past week and a half. You've been working yourself overtime, and you say you need practice!" He shook his head. "Something's wrong. I saw it the first day you tried to stand." Joan frowned at him.

"Nothing is wrong," she said.

"Is it your left leg?" Kurt asked. Joan raised her head quickly to look at him. "I've noticed every time you try walking on that foot, you never manage." Joan looked away. So he had noticed and knew. "Joan, why don't you tell someone?" Kurt asked.

"I'm not going to be a burden!" Joan snapped. "I've been a burden ever since I came here!" She bit back the words. She had said too much.

"A burden?" Kurt asked. "Mother is glad you're here. She's been broken ever since Eliza died five years back. She was your age. Since you've come, it's almost like Mother has been healed." Joan didn't say anything. "Plus, you've helped out much more than we ever thought you would," Kurt continued. "Pa has enjoyed having you around too. He loved Eliza just as much as Ma and was so proud of her. When she died, a piece of him died too. But since you've come along, it's as though some of that piece has come back." Joan sat still, looking at her hands. She couldn't say anything. "Here," Kurt said, standing up. "I have an idea." He walked over and held out his arm. "Now stand up." Joan struggled to get her legs over the edge of the bed and took his arm, then raised herself wobbly to her right foot. "Now take a step on your right foot and lean on my arm like you'd lean on your left leg." Joan did, and for the first time in two long weeks, took one tiny, scuffling step. "Now instead of trying to lift your left foot, just drag it up next to your right one." Joan took a deep breath and tried. To her surprise and almost delight, she was able to. "Now lean on my arm again and take a step with your right foot," Kurt instructed. Joan did as he said. Then again, she dragged her left foot forward. Slowly, with Kurt's help, she made a round of the kitchen table and then slumped exhausted back onto her bed. Kurt sat down at the table again. "Now I will make you a crutch so you can move around on your own, but you have to tell the others in the morning." Joan looked down. "Or I will tell them if you don't." Joan looked up and shook her head. "In the morning, promise?" Joan nodded mutely. "Good night, then." He stood up and went out.

Joan didn't sleep well that night. In the morning, everyone would know. So she was lying awake when Martha came down to make breakfast. "Good morning, Joan." She smiled and stirred up the fire then walked over and sat down beside Joan's bed. "How do you feel, Joan?"

Joan smiled. "Fine."

"You seem a little pale. Are you sure?" Joan nodded. Martha smiled, then stood up. "Do you want something to eat or drink?"

Joan shook her head. "Not now. I'm fine." Martha looked worried but said nothing. After a while, Captain Hood and Jamerson came down. Jamerson looked toward her then went to the small mirror and began to comb his hair. A few minutes later, Kurt entered. He looked at Joan as if asking if she had told them. But she shook her head slightly. The family sat down for breakfast. Kurt turned to look at her, as though warning her that he would tell if she didn't, so she gulped, then said, "I have something to say." Everyone turned toward her in complete surprise. "It's about my not walking," Joan said. She saw Martha and Captain Hood look at each other and then back at her.

"Go on," Martha said after a moment.

Joan looked down at her hands and then said, "My left leg is crippled and won't hold my weight." Martha gasped, and silence fell over the room heavily. Joan looked up. Jamerson's face was as white as a sheet, and he was staring at her in surprise and hurt. Captain Hood was staring at his hands with unseeing eyes, and Martha was staring at her with wide eyes, her hands tightly clenched together. "Kurt said he'd make me a crutch so I will be able to be up and about in a few days," Joan said. She looked straight at Martha. "Meanwhile, I'll take on all the mending, sewing, and knitting. Also, small jobs such as peeling vegetables and folding wash."

Suddenly, Jamerson seemed to snap out of his shock. "What do you mean, Kurt? Do you mean you told Kurt before me?" His voice was strained.

"Now Jamerson," Joan said softly. "I didn't tell him. He guessed."

Jamerson looked over at Kurt. "Why didn't you tell me?" he asked.

"I thought she should," Kurt said.

Jamerson shook his head. "Why didn't you tell me sooner, Joan?"

Joan looked down at her hands. "I'm not going to be a burden."

Martha gasped again then said, "Oh Joan, you're not a burden," after a moment. "Can't you see that?" Joan looked down and then slowly shook her head. Martha looked desperately at Captain Hood but said nothing.

Five days later, Kurt presented her with her crutch. Joan thought it was beautiful. It was made of white pine. Kurt had engraved vines and flowers from the top all the way down to the handhold. He'd covered the top and handhold with soft white leather. The bottom he'd covered in grippy leather. Joan took it with a bright smile. "What do you want for it?" she asked.

Kurt shook his head. "You just learn to walk." Joan smiled and then stood up shakily from the bed, slipping the crutch under her left arm. It was perfect. It took a couple of tumbles and a whole week before she was comfortable with it, but she was adjusting fine.

Within two weeks, Joan had adjusted very well. Once again, she was up earlier than the family and had breakfast ready when they came down. Captain Hood made a ramp instead of steps from the back door into the yard. Still, there were many things Joan couldn't do, so she took on all the spinning, carding, and weaving. Anything she could to make herself useful. The months passed slowly, and the harbor began to melt, and then it was time for Captain Hood to repair his ship and head back out to sea. This time, Kurt would be going along.

Joan stood, leaning on her crutch, and watched as Martha and Jamerson followed Captain Hood and Kurt to the wharf. The *Martha* was sailing that day. Joan turned back to the dishes she needed to finish. She worked quietly, standing on her right leg while her crutch leaned against the table. Martha said that they would put in the garden the next day, and Joan could hardly wait. There was a knock on the door, and Joan called, "Come in." The front door opened, and a moment later, Molly stood at the door. Joan smiled.

Molly walked over and sat down at the table. "So the *Martha* sailed," Joan nodded. "What are you planning to do this spring?"

Joan shrugged and smiled. "I'm not sure. I'm just trying to take one day at a time."

Molly smiled and then asked, "This morning I heard Uncle Victor talking." Molly waited a moment, then continued, "It was about the rebels." Joan looked up quickly. "So from what Uncle Victor said, the Virginian assembly sets up its own eleven-man Committee of Correspondence. I'm not sure what it means, but he said he's sure others will soon follow. He seemed quite excited about it, actually."

Joan smiled. "I'm glad."

"But what does it mean?" Molly asked, perplexed.

"I'm guessing those men in Virginia set up their own type of government, you might say."

Molly frowned slightly. "I'm thinking that if other colonies follow, there could be trouble." Joan nodded and tried to seem worried, but her pulse quickened, and she almost hoped it would stir up trouble.

Joan sat across the table from Jamerson, listening to him read out of a book of Captain Hood's. He was a great reader, and she worked on her sewing while he read. Martha sat in a rocker nearby, listening quietly while she sewed a button on Jamerson's new shirt. The house seemed empty without Kurt and Captain Hood, but none of them said anything. After about a half hour, Jamerson closed the book, and Joan looked up from her sewing to smile. Martha had fallen asleep by then. "You're a great reader, Jamerson," Joan said quietly.

Jamerson smiled. "Thank you," he said.

Joan laid her sewing in her lap. "Do you miss Kurt?"

Jamerson nodded. "He's like my big brother."

Joan smiled gently. "I know."

Jamerson smiled at her. "Someday you'll understand."

Joan laughed softly. "Perhaps," she said. "Now you'd better get to bed."

Jamerson nodded and put the book away. Then Martha woke up and climbed the stairs to her own room while Joan went to her bed in the corner. She slept in the kitchen now since she couldn't climb the stairs.

So the summer and fall came and went, and soon winter was upon them. Captain Hood and Kurt came back, and the *Martha* was once again settled in the harbor to wait out winter.

Chapter 11

Joan sat before the fire. A cold wind was rising. December was cold, and she shivered. She hoped winter would pass soon. Martha was mixing together a batch of cornbread while Joan mended a hole in Kurt's sock. Suddenly, the door banged open, and Kurt and Jamerson came in, howling with what seemed like delight. "My word!" Martha cried, almost dropping her spoon in the corn mixture. "What in the world, boys? What is going on?"

Kurt held up a newspaper, his eyes twinkling. "Guess what, Ma?" He chuckled. "Some Boston men and boys went and threw 340 chests of tea overboard into the Boston Harbor!"

Martha gasped, and her eyes widened. Joan lifted her head, and her eyes began to dance. "340 chests?" Martha asked in a low voice.

Jamerson and Kurt grinned. "Yup, and only one man was arrested," Jamerson said.

Martha stared at them. "How many men were involved?"

"All we know of were 170."

Martha shook her head a bit weakly. "But how did they not get recognized?"

Jamerson grinned broadly. "They dressed up like Indians." Joan couldn't hold back the suppressed giggle.

They all turned to look at her. "Joan!" Martha said in surprise. "Surely you don't think this is funny?"

Joan choked back a giggle and smiled. "Indeed, ma'am, I do. Quite funny, as a matter of fact!" Martha shook her head, and the boys grinned at her approvingly. Jamerson took the newspaper from Kurt and walked over to sit down by Joan. He then read the story out loud. It was short because many details hadn't reached them just yet. Joan smiled as she listened, a strange excitement filling her. Martha listened too, growing more and more aghast.

Kurt chuckled at her face and threw approving glances in Joan's direction.

"Just wait and see. England will have the last say in this!" Martha said.

Martha said at last. She sighed as she placed the cornbread near the fire. "This spells T-R-O-U-B-L-E. Trouble!"

Kurt tossed his head lightly. "Who cares?" He suddenly became serious. "I say bring on the trouble. War if need be. I'm sixteen now, and I'll throw away ropes and sails and take up firearms if that means freedom."

Martha whirled on him. "What happens if you get one of your limbs blown off? What will you say then? Will it be worth being half a man?"

Kurt straightened indignantly but said quietly, "Yes."

For a moment, the two pairs of gray eyes held, then Martha turned away, and Joan saw the tears. "It isn't worth it for me," she said.

Joan reached for her crutch. "Did you bring the salt we sent you for, Kurt?" She asked, trying to change the subject.

Kurt nodded. "Oh yeah. Here it is." He opened his coat and handed the bag of salt to her.

"Thank you."

Later that day, Joan sat in the kitchen carding a batch of wool when Kurt came in. Jamerson was in his room studying, and Martha had gone for a walk. Kurt dragged up a chair and sat down next to her, beginning to pull wads of wool off the tangle of gray wool in the basket. "What do you think of this Boston Tea Party, as they call it?" he asked after a moment. "Really. I know you think it is funny, but what do you really think of it?"

Joan didn't say anything for a moment, only carded a few more balls of wool. Then she said softly, "Well, the British have been unjustly taxing us. I think those men and boys in Boston did right to throw the tea over into the bay. It wasn't that they really wanted to hurt the British, I think, just simply tell them what paper and pleading hasn't been able to. Simply we want our freedom, and if it starts a war, then I say go to it." She stopped there, her face flushing a bit because she had said too much.

But Kurt grinned, and his eyes twinkled. "I'm sure what you say is true. It's a shame you weren't born in America. I guess, for now, you're just an English rebel."

Joan began to laugh then. "The phrases you come up with!" she said at last with a smile. "An English rebel, indeed!" Kurt stood up with a grin and left the room, whistling quietly.

*****

It was now April 4, 1774. Joan was now almost sixteen. She had spent nearly two years at the Hoods'. Jamerson was fourteen. He had grown. He now stood three inches over her. Over the two years, he had lost his clinginess to her and relied more upon Kurt. Joan said nothing of this, though sometimes it hurt because she still loved him just the same and wanted only the very best for him. Captain Hood and Kurt would be leaving port in just another week.

Joan was weeding the garden when she saw Kurt and Jamerson walking up the street toward the house, fast. They were talking in raised voices, and their voices sounded angry. She reached for her crutch and raised herself to her feet, going into the kitchen just as the front door banged. Not waiting to take off their shoes, the two boys stormed into the kitchen talking angrily. "Joan, where is Ma?" Kurt asked. Joan nodded toward the parlor. "Airing out the company room." Kurt headed for the door of the parlor. "Ma," Joan heard him say, "Can I talk to you for a moment?" Martha came out to the kitchen. "Here it is," Kurt said. His face was drawn tight, and his eyes snapped with anger. "Those wretched British have closed the port to Boston. They're trying to starve the Bostonians into repentance!" Martha gasped, and Joan grew tense. "Father is talking to the town committee right now. What we are going to do is take a trip with fully loaded carts and wagons from this town down to Boston. We can go over the land outlet into Boston."

Martha nodded. "So?"

"We need every family to give something."

Martha nodded. "Of course. We have plenty. Joan, get those heavy hampers out of the hall closet."

A week later, three fully loaded wagons stood in the town square, filled with food and supplies. The Hoods had given liberally. Kurt was to drive one wagon. The night before the wagons were to pull out, Kurt and Captain Hood sat at the table making last-minute plans. "It should take you about two weeks to get there. Don't take more than three days to unload. Then sell off the wagons if you can and get back here. By then, I'll have finished up those last-minute repairs on the Martha I put off this week and have loaded her up. Don't take longer than you must," Captain Hood said. Kurt nodded.

Joan listened intently. If the truth be told, she really did want to see an American city. "Is Boston very big?" she asked. Both Kurt and Captain Hood looked up then, almost in disbelief.

"It's one of the biggest cities in America," Kurt said.

Captain Hood opened his mouth to say something, then turned to Kurt. "I say, lad, why don't you take Joan here with you?"

Joan opened her mouth to protest, but Kurt grinned. "That's a smashing idea!" He turned sharply toward her. "Would you like to go?" Joan looked hesitant and doubtful. But Martha cut in.

"Go on, Joan. This will be your big chance to see Boston. It's a beautiful city, you see! I can handle things here."

As though to clinch the hesitation, Captain Hood said, "This summer, I'll take Jamerson on one of my trips to make up for him not going this time if you'll go." Joan looked across the room at her brother's face and was lost.

*****

"There you go," Captain Hood said the next morning in the twilight before sunrise as he lifted Joan to the wagon seat.

"Godspeed," Martha said.

Jamerson held up her crutch. "Have lots of fun," he said with a grin. Joan smiled and took her crutch. Kurt climbed up beside her. "Bye, see you in a month!" Martha said.

Captain Hood clapped his hand over his son's knee then stood back. "Godspeed."

Families of the other two drivers called along with the Hoods and Jamerson. Joan waved. Then slowly, the town fell behind, and she sighed. Her pulse quickened, and she stared around her at the landscape washed in the early morning light.

Kurt looked over at her and grinned. "Excited?" he asked.

Joan nodded. "I guess I am."

Kurt smiled. "You know, this is the first time I've been away from home alone by myself."

Joan looked up in surprise. "Really?" she asked.

He nodded, reaching to pull back slightly on the brake as they neared a small hill. "You might say I'm barely getting out into the world. Considering that last year was my first summer on the seas, and this my first time away from home alone." Joan smiled. It was hard to imagine that, considering that he had just turned seventeen. Suddenly before them, a deer bolted across the road. Kurt cursed softly as he tried to steady the startled horses. "Danged critter!" he muttered, fiddling with the lines.

"I thought it was pretty," Joan said.

"Huh! So you would, but you're not holding the reins!" Kurt snapped as he finally managed to get the team settled down.

Joan laughed. "I doubt it's hard." She peeked around the edge of the wagon to see if the other drivers were having trouble. Kurt only grunted.

Joan was glad when they stopped for the night. She was sore from head to toe from the bouncing wagon. Finally, the wagons circled up, and Kurt jumped down. "Hold on!" he said as Joan tossed her crutch over the edge and swung her right leg over as though to get down. "You'll hurt yourself." He walked around and helped her down, then began to unhitch the horses.

One man started a fire, and soon the three men were busy making camp preparations. They did let Joan do the cooking. Then one man took out his fiddle and played. Kurt took up a map to study it, and the last man smoked lazily on his pipe. Joan washed the dishes and stacked them near the fire. Afterward, she sat down next to Kurt and peered at his map. She couldn't tell what it was supposed to mean. There were so many lines and small words written all over it. Kurt looked up as Joan cocked her head, trying to make heads or tails of the lined thing. He chuckled and tapped the map.

"This is one of the most complicated maps I've ever read if that's a comfort to you." Joan smiled.

"Indeed, it is! I couldn't tell a river from a road!" Kurt chuckled. "That's why men do the traveling," he said. His eyes twinkled with amusement.

"Not either!" Joan cried indignantly.

Kurt chuckled. "Name me one woman explorer," he said.

"Well, there's…and there's…" Joan stammered then said firmly, "There's a lot of them." Kurt and the other men burst out into a roar of laughter. Joan smiled sheepishly and shook her head.

It was a long and fun two weeks. Joan enjoyed it tremendously. Not five days into their journey, they met other carts and wagons headed for Boston. So they were in a train when they finally reached Boston. Joan sat wide-eyed as she watched the city around her. The place was buzzing. But for every civilian, there were three Redcoat soldiers. Joan frowned slightly. She didn't like the sight of them. She looked at Kurt. His face was twisted into a frown, and he looked as though he could spit. She couldn't help but laugh heartily. He looked around at her and glared. "What's so blasted funny?" he asked.

"You!" Joan choked at last.

"What about me?" Kurt snapped.

"Your face is so terribly funny! Forgive me for laughing, but it is so funny!" And her mouth twisted slightly over the compressed laughter.

"Humph!" Kurt snorted but grinned sheepishly. They were directed to a place where the supplies could be unloaded. "I should have dropped you off at a boarding house," Kurt told her. "Because unloading will be dreadfully boring. It will take at least two hours to get the first wagon unloaded, which is all we can do today."

Joan shrugged. "I don't mind."

Chapter 12

But soon she did mind, just after half an hour had passed. She was sitting there, looking around at her surroundings when she heard her name called. "Joan." She looked toward Kurt, but he was busy and couldn't have called her. Besides, that wasn't his voice. "Joan." She turned again, and her eyes settled on a tall Redcoat standing nearby. Something about him was familiar. He grinned. "Don't you recognize me?"

She recognized him then. "David Nel!" she cried in amazement. "Fancy seeing you here!"

He chuckled. "Fancy seeing yourself here," he said, walking over. Joan shook her head.

"I thought you were still in training."

"So I was until I was shipped over here last winter."

Joan smiled. "Then you were here when the tea was thrown into the harbor?"

"Much to my distress," he muttered. Joan laughed. "So when did you come over, and how in the world did you afford it?"

Joan laughed in delight. "I didn't have to pay, I mean money. Jamerson and I came over by mistake."

"How is the little kid, anyways?" David Nel asked, shifting the rifle over his shoulder.

"Fine, grown so much. He's taller than me now. He didn't come to Boston though."

David grinned. "I always knew he would grow big. He had the build of a boy that wasn't going to be puny. Does he still cling to you like death?"

A shadow of sadness passed for an instant over Joan's face. "No."

David raised an eyebrow. "He got too big for ya, eh?"

"Oh no!" Joan said hurriedly. "It's just that there is this boy that he thinks of as his brother." She nodded toward Kurt. "That's the boy." David looked toward Kurt.

"Oh. Then how did you get to America?"

Joan shook her head. "You do ask so many questions! What about you? Have you heard from your family?"

David nodded. "I've gotten letters. I do know they were greatly distressed when you stopped showing up." David now, was the baker's, who Joan had worked for in England, son.

"I supposed they would be," Joan said quietly. "So what do you think of America?" she asked after a moment.

"Oh, it's great," David said sarcastically. "Especially when even the children make wide circles around you."

"Oh, I'm sorry," Joan said.

"No, really, the people aren't that bad, and Boston's actually a great city," David said.

"Have you seen it?"

Joan smiled. "Everything I've seen has been from this wagon seat."

"Oh well then, let me show you around," David said.

Joan hesitated. "I don't know," she said quietly, glancing toward Kurt.

"Oh, poppycock!" David said. "Come along. I'll only take half an hour at the most."

Joan sighed. "Very well. Only half an hour."

He grinned. Joan reached down and picked up her crutch and held it out to him. "What's…" He stopped in surprise and looked up at her. "What happened?" he asked after a minute of shock.

"A fever really laid me low, so they told me."

David whistled softly. "It must have!"

"Do you still want to show me the sights?"

David grinned. "If you feel up to it."

Joan smiled and nodded. "Alright, if you don't mind walking with a cripple." David grinned again and helped her down from the wagon.

They walked in silence for a moment, then David asked, "Does it hurt?"

Joan laughed. "Sometimes, but not today." David sighed with relief. He began to show her around.

After about twenty minutes, he took her to a small inn and ordered a cup of tea for each of them. "David," Joan said quietly. "Not tea for me, please. Coffee."

His head whipped around then in surprise. "Coffee?" he asked. Joan nodded.

"I guess I better tell you now. I've turned rebel, or Yankee."

David stared at her with unbelieving eyes for a second. He asked in a shocked voice, "Why? I mean, you come from England. Why did you turn Yankee?"

Joan sighed quietly. "David, what you say is true. I did come from England, but not the one you know. I came from corners and alleys where people scuttle around like rats! Where to go hungry for nearly twenty-four hours and to bed dressed in rags was no new thing. Where every Sunday, I had to carry two buckets of water up seven flights of stairs three or four times just to have a bath. Do you realize it wasn't until I came to America that I touched a flower? Also, that I got a full eight hours of sleep every night?" David was listening with respectful silence. "Maybe if things hadn't turned out so well for Jamerson and me, then I wouldn't be so eager to turn against England. But David, America has given me everything I ever wanted! My heritage, love and trust, friendship, and most of all, and what I thank God for the most, is that it has made Jamerson so happy! He can live like every other boy! Go to schools, have friends, and most of all, dream his dreams and have a chance they shall come true." Joan looked quietly up at David. "We had nothing in England but filth and loneliness! Nothing but rats and scurrying people. America is grand, and I beg your pardon if this is an insult, but if there is a war, America shall win because the American people are proud and stubborn. They'll fight until the last man if it means freedom. They're just rough farmers and sailors, most of them, but heaven knows how proud they are of this new land they could make into the finest country the world has ever known."

David sighed quietly. "You almost guilt me for being British," he said quietly.

"You needn't be. We each have our beliefs, and if we believe they are right, then we must stand for them," Joan said. Then she laughed. "Do you realize I've talked more today than I have in the last two months, I dare say!"

David looked at her in surprise. "Really?" he asked.

Joan nodded. "The Hoods would be perfectly shocked. They are the family Jamerson and I live with. That boy you saw at the unloading yard was their son, Kurt. He's an alright fellow."

David smiled. The maid brought the tea then, and David said to her, "Sorry, miss, but I guess this young lady would rather have coffee." The maid left, and David turned to Joan. "So what do you think of Boston so far?"

Joan beamed. "It's just perfectly lovely!" David smiled, pleased.

It was not half an hour later when David walked a weary Joan back to the wagon, but one full hour. "I hope I didn't tire you out," David said when he at last stood beside the wagon with her.

"Oh no, I enjoyed it," Joan said. Then David helped her back up onto the wagon seat and said his goodbyes.

"Joan!" Joan turned to see Kurt walking fast toward the wagon. "Where have you been?" he asked.

"Seeing Boston," Joan said quietly.

"With that soldier?" Kurt asked coldly.

"Yes, Kurt, he's…"

"How could you?" Kurt interrupted in an angry tone.

"How could I do what?" Joan asked.

"Let a red lobster show you Boston like he owns it!" Kurt said.

"Mr. Hood, we've finished over here. Good night," a sturdy man called from where they had been stacking crates and barrels. Kurt waved then clambered onto the wagon seat. Joan pinched her lips together. If he was so opinionated, then she needn't spend her breath trying to explain.

What a rough three days it was for Joan. Kurt didn't go a day without letting her know how wrong she had been to let a Redcoat soldier show her Boston. But at last, the one remaining wagon they would travel back in pulled out of Boston, and Joan was glad. Maybe she didn't like traveling after all.

Two or three days passed on the trail, and still, Kurt clung firmly to his opinion that she shouldn't have done what she had done. Joan was getting fed up. She got that he didn't like the British, but he did carry it too far! On the fourth day, Kurt started up again. Joan was so fed up that she almost shouted at him. Instead, she picked up her crutch, threw it over the edge of the wagon, and said calmly, "I'll walk from here."

"Huh?" Kurt stared at her blankly.

"I'll walk from here. Kindly stop the wagon." Kurt shook his head, a little baffled, and stopped the horses.

"Now what are you going to do?" he asked.

"Walk," Joan said.

"Walk?" Kurt repeated.

"Yes."

"All the way home?" Joan shook her head.

"I'll stop at the first farm along the way and find work. From there, who knows what'll happen." Kurt pushed his tricorn back and shook his head slightly in a baffled way.

"Have you gone crazy?" he asked.

"No," Joan said.

"Then why in the world are you just jumping off and heading out like this?"

"Because I'm sick to death of being preached at! You'd think I committed murder! That 'red lobster' was David Nel, a friend of mine I used to know in England. I didn't even realize he had been shipped over here. I haven't seen him in probably five years. He simply wanted to show me around! I told him I was a rebel, and he accepted the fact!"

Kurt stared at her. "A friend of yours," he mused after a moment, then nodded. "Oh, I see. I'll grab your crutch." Joan shook her head and glared at him. But he ignored her and went back for her crutch.

*****

Joan was glad to get back and to settle back into normal. Of course, both Martha and Molly wanted every detail of her visit to Boston the day after they arrived back home. Captain Hood and Kurt set back out to sea. Jamerson would go on the next trip. So the days passed until two weeks had come, when something so extraordinary happened. Joan had a very difficult time believing it.

Joan was weeding in the flower bed behind the house when she heard Martha call almost excitedly from the door. "Joan, come in here." Joan picked up her crutch, lifted herself painfully to her feet, and hobbled in. "There are two men in the company room who want to see you," Martha said quietly when Joan came into the kitchen. With a small frown, Joan started toward the company room door. When she opened it, she saw a tall, genial old man sitting in an armchair, lighting an ivory pipe. Another, much younger man, about nineteen, stood before the hearth, looking at his pocket watch. Both looked up when she opened the door. The old man came instantly to his feet, snuffing out his pipe. The younger man put his watch into his pocket. Both seemed a bit surprised and a little pleased. "Miss Rindle, I presume?" the old man asked, stepping forward and holding out his hand. For a moment, Joan's mind went blank, then she remembered. Her name was Rindle. She nodded, bobbing slightly and shaking the man's hand. "How do you do?" asked the old man with a smile.

Joan smiled a bit herself. "Fine. Thank you. May I ask your name?"

"Surely. My name is Alford Drew Beesly. This is my friend Jeremiah Donald Rindle."

Joan started and looked at the young man. He had blue eyes and blond hair. His skin was sun-tanned so brown it was darker than his hair. He bowed a little. "I am your father's cousin, Miss. So maybe your cousin once taken away or something of the sort." Joan stared at him.

"Miss Rindle, I must ask you a few questions before we get carried away," the old man said, throwing a reproving glance at the younger man. Joan nodded and sunk into a chair. Mr. Beesly took a leather case from the floor by his chair and opened it. From it, he drew a sheaf of papers. "Your name is Joan Anna Rindle, correct?"

Joan nodded. "Yes, sir."

"You do have a brother, correct?"

"Yes, sir."

"His name?"

"Jamerson."

The old man smiled in a pleased way and then asked, "What were the names of your parents?"

"Elanor May and John Havre Rindle," Joan answered.

The man seemed even more pleased. "How old are you?"

"Sixteen."

"How old is your brother?"

"Fourteen."

"How old were you when your parents died?"

"Seven."

"Your brother?"

"Five."

Mr. Beesly smiled and rubbed his chin. "Well now, Miss Rindle, it appears we have found you at last."

Joan stared at him. "What do you mean?" she asked.

Mr. Beesly looked up at Mr. Rindle. "Won't you tell her, sir?"

The young man nodded and took a chair opposite Joan. "Some years ago, there was this very wealthy family in England. Two brothers were born to it, both strong and healthy. But one was quite opinionated. He believed he should choose what he wanted and for the most part made wise and good choices. Everybody was usually happy. But when this brother was about twenty, he married a milkmaid from a poor farm in the country. This so enraged the family that he was disowned and told never to contact them again. But the second brother, who was the youngest, loved his brother dearly, but no amount of talking could change the mind of his parents. The first brother then fled the country with his young bride. They went to Switzerland where they settled down to raise a family. Their first child was a daughter, and their second was a little boy. Afterward, they had two more pretty daughters. Time marched on, and the boy grew up and was married. Then he left Switzerland, taking his wife with him. His older sister begged to come along. Neither knew that their father had been born in England. This young man, it may interest you to know, was named John. He settled down in a small London side street. He was never very wealthy, and he and his wife lived very humble lives. They had two children, a daughter and a son. It may also interest you to know that those two are you and your brother."

Joan started. Her eyes were wide in surprise. "Yes, you are from the blood of one of the wealthiest families in England. Your grandfather's parents died not more than ten years ago. They were both very old. Now your great uncle has received the family title and fortune. The first thing he did after receiving these was to start a hunt for his brother. He knew from scant and short notes from his brother that he lived in Switzerland. But when men and horses were sent to fetch your grandfather, the men found that he and his wife had died. The two youngest daughters could not be traced. After a few inquiries, your great-uncle found that your father had moved to London. By then it was too late. Your father and mother had been dead for nearly six months, and you and your brother could not be found. My father searched London, and to his surprise, he found your aunt on her deathbed where he learned from her that she happened to know of a certain Captain Hood who had been looking for the parents of two children, who had rare qualities. You, your eyes. Your brother, the hair color. Within a week, my father had sold the family estate in England and moved to New York, here in America, where he has continued the family trade. But a fever laid him low before he left England, along with the worrying and anxiety. So when we reached America, he handed the searching over to me. This was all about two years ago. Since then, I and my trustful lawyer here have been going up and down the American shores looking for one Captain Hood, or at least where he lives. Finally, we found out from a man about twenty miles down the shoreline. Here in town, it was no trouble contacting the house where the captain lives. His wife told us that, indeed, two children lived with them, and we have at last found you."

Joan couldn't believe what she was hearing. Everything was in shambles. It wasn't sinking in right away. "Maybe I'd better tell you in plain English," Jeremiah Donald Rindle said. "Now you see, my father has all this money, which should have gone to your grandfather, only your grandfather was disowned. So when my grandparents died, my father vowed to give back the money to his brother or his family. Which means you and your brother." Joan stared, her eyes wide with sudden understanding.

"Oh no!" she cried. "Your father must keep the money. Jamerson and I could never take it!"

Jeremiah Donald Rindle grinned. "Explain to my father. He told me if I ever found you, then to bring you to him." Joan put her head in her hand and moaned softly. Everything was so complicated!

"Miss Rindle, may we meet your brother? After all, being the only male grandson of Edward Dell Rindle that we can trace, he will in time inherit all money and titles," Mr. Beesly said.

Joan raised her head in a shocked air. "Oh no! He's never had to handle money business. He's never known much worry and trouble. I've tried to keep his life as carefree as possible, but I'm afraid I haven't done a very good job of it." Mr. Beesly looked at his young employer.

"We'd like to meet the boy all the same," Mr. Rindle said. Joan nodded mutely and picked up her crutch.

At the bottom of the stairs, she called, "Jamerson, please come down here for a moment. There is a matter of importance to discuss with you."

A few minutes later, Jamerson came bounding down the stairs. Joan led him into the company room. The story was explained again, and the reason for the two men being there. "Great thunder!" Jamerson whistled at last. He seemed pleased. "That's a great honor." The two men smiled and leaned back in their chairs. "But I can't accept," Jamerson said quietly.

"Why not?" Mr. Beesly asked, sitting up with a start.

"Joan and I have lived with very little money in our lives and have made out alright. Besides, we haven't earned it." Jamerson looked over at Joan and smiled. "Also, Great Uncle might disown us himself if he knew what we were." Both men sat forward in interest.

"What do you mean?" asked Mr. Rindle.

"We've turned Yankee," Jamerson said, and Joan nodded.

"Well." A slow smile touched the corners of Mr. Rindle's mouth. "You don't say. I did myself after about a year of being over here. Father, of course, did not agree, but he took it as a fact. He will do the same for you. Now we have a neat little vessel waiting in the harbor, and we sail right down to New York and let you meet my father."

Joan and Jamerson looked at each other. "We must talk to Martha," Joan said quietly.

Chapter 13

Two weeks later, a neat little vessel sailed into the harbor, bearing with it a sixteen-year-old girl and a boy about fourteen, accompanied by two large men dressed finely. Thirty minutes later, a fine carriage pulled up to a large house in the finest part of New York, and the two children were escorted quickly and solemnly to a large and dark study where an old man sat at a desk, working over some sheets of paper.

Joan felt sure Mr. Rindle and Mr. Beesly would hear her heart beating as she limped down the hall, her crutch making more noise than she liked. Mr. Beesly stepped to the door and opened it, saying, "Sir, your great-niece and nephew." Then Joan stepped into the doorway.

An old man rose from a chair behind the desk, and a bright and gentle smile spread over his old face. "Yes, you are Edward's grandchildren," he said and walked around the table as Joan and Jamerson stepped forward. He smiled as he looked at Joan. "You have his eyes and confounded stubborn tilt of the chin." Joan blushed slightly and looked down. "And you, boy, you have his build and hair color. You'll be just like him." Jamerson shuffled a bit and smiled. "Now please have a seat." Joan and Jamerson took a seat in the two chairs offered to them. Their uncle walked over behind the desk and sat down. "Now maybe my son hasn't told you, but my name is Jeremiah. But you may just call me Uncle. It would be best. Now Jeremiah Jr., my son, must have explained to you the story of your heritage." Joan and Jamerson nodded.

"Yes, sir," Jamerson said. "And we'd rather not have the money."

Their uncle started in surprise. "What?" he asked.

Jamerson nodded and explained. "Well, I'll be," muttered the old man at last.

An hour later, Joan and Jamerson were shown to their rooms. Joan's room was as large as the Hood's kitchen. The bed was huge and soft. There were soft rugs everywhere. Huge windows overlooked a pretty garden. Joan stared about her at her surroundings with wide eyes. "I'll fetch some hot water, ma'am," the maid who had shown her to her room said, curtsying. Joan nodded, too dazed to really tell what the maid had said. She went to the window, lifted the sash, and looked out. There was a rose bush nearby, and the scent was strong and pretty.

Joan reached out and plucked off a rose. There was a tap on the door, and she called, "Come in." The door opened, and the maid came in followed by another with two steaming buckets of water. Behind her was another maid with another two buckets. Behind her came a maid carrying a set of towels, and behind her came yet another maid carrying what seemed like a dress. The first maid opened a door to the right, and the maids went in. Joan reached for her crutch, hobbled over, and looked in. It was a bathroom. A large white tub stood at one end of the room. The room was wallpapered in white with small and pretty pink roses. At the other end of the room was a large vanity table with numerous odd objects. Near the tub was another smaller table with several bottles and a sponge on it. The maid with the towels was hanging them near the tub, while the maids with the water were pouring them into the tub. The maid with the dress was hanging it up on a hook by the vanity table. Joan saw that it wasn't just a dress, but petticoats and undergarments had been hidden beneath it.

These were set out, and the first maid turned to Joan. "Your bath is ready, ma'am. Just ring the bell there by the tub if you need anything at all."

Joan smiled. "Thank you," she said quietly. The maids bobbed their curtsies and left. Joan had never known there could be soaps that smelled as good as the ones by the tub. They smelled like roses. She washed her hair. It was now quite long and hung down to her knees, a shimmering mass. She took her bath and then dressed in the garments set out. The dress was of satin or some smooth cloth of the sort. White and turquoise. When at last she stood before the mirror, she found out just how well it matched her complexion. She was delighted. Her hair was not quite dry, so she rang the bell.

A few minutes later, the maid appeared. "Yes'm?" she asked, bobbing a curtsy.

Joan smiled. "How do you get rid of the water in the tub? It's completely too heavy for me to carry if I could carry it."

The maid smiled. "The maids do that," Joan frowned slightly.

"But you've already done so much!"

The maid smiled again. "We get paid, Miss." Joan smiled.

"Oh, so it's like your work?" The maid nodded. "Oh well then, I won't feel so bad about it then." The maid smiled. "Your uncle said when you were finished, he'd like to dine with you and your brother."

Joan had never tasted such a meal as was set on her uncle's table. When she entered the dining room, she was nearly blinded by the light shimmering off the silver candle holders, silverware, and clasps on the chairs. Her uncle stood before his place at one end of the table, and Jamerson stood at a chair nearby. They were talking hotly. "The King is a selfish old!" Jamerson was saying.

"Boy!" bellowed their uncle in a rage. "You'd better mind your manners!"

Joan froze at the door, still leaning on her crutch. "The king is your sovereign!"

"God is my sovereign!" Jamerson said, his body growing straight. For a moment, he looked like a man, staring coldly back at his uncle. "God is the only man I shall ever kneel to!"

Uncle's hand came down with a bang that made the dishes rattle. "England gave America life!"

"England did not! They may have sent men over here, but they have left America alone for too many years!"

"What about the war with the French? Tell me why you renegades won!"

"We had the help of the English, but we are being unfairly taxed by men we did not vote into court!" Jamerson growled.

"Blasted taxes! Is that all you blasted rebels can talk about?" Uncle said.

"No, we can talk about freedom, and being treated equally, and not having a blasted, good-for-nothing, bloated hog for a king!"

Uncle now literally raged, his face turning red. Suddenly, Joan felt a hand on her shoulder and looked up. Jeremiah stood behind her. He cleared his throat loudly, and Uncle and Jamerson turned toward them. Instantly, Uncle pulled himself together and bowed stiffly.

"Joan, how very pretty you look. Please have a seat."

Joan moved forward into the room. She took a seat opposite Jamerson. After a moment of tense silence, Joan said, "Uncle, do you have any paintings of our grandfather?"

Her uncle smiled. "Yes indeed, I do. I shall show you some when we finish eating." The meal was less tense afterward, and Joan tried to keep her uncle talking about her grandfather.

Afterward, he took them into a long drawing room where the walls were hung with paintings. He led them to where several paintings of the same young man hung. Joan started. Back to her flashed a memory, almost forgotten. A young man with a face like the one that peered at her from the painting before her. She remembered walking by the side of this young man while the busy streets of London buzzed around them. Her grandfather? Was her uncle sure that this painting wasn't her father? But even as she looked, she knew it had to be her grandfather. Her father had had higher cheekbones and a cleaner-cut jawline. Jamerson was still as he looked at the man in the picture. Joan glanced from him to the painting. Yes, Jamerson was very much like the man in the painting and like the young man in her memory. They walked about the room while Mr. Rindle explained about different paintings.

After a few minutes, a maid came to the door, saying that there was a man there to see Mr. Rindle. "Jeremiah, do continue for me," Joan's uncle said, placing a hand on his son's shoulder.

"Yes, sir," Jeremiah said, and Mr. Rindle left the room. As soon as the door shut, Jeremiah turned to Jamerson. "Listen, I'm not preaching, just giving some advice," he said in a low, calm voice. "I know my father, and you have two very different opinions about America and England, but you must keep yours to yourself. The same as I have to. My father will just continue to argue until you both can't abide one another! It happened to me two years ago."

Jamerson frowned a bit but nodded. "Alright," he said. "But that doesn't mean I will give up my opinions!"

Jeremiah grinned. "I know."

Then he continued to show them the paintings and explain about their past. After a while, the door opened, and Mr. Rindle came in. "Joan, my dear, that was my good friend Leon David Fallo. He suggested that he bring over his three daughters to meet you. Of course, I accepted for you. I have already given orders that a tea party shall be arranged in the front parlor. Tomorrow at three." Joan gulped a trifle. This was not starting out to her liking.

When Joan opened the door to her room two hours later, she saw the maid she had left before dinner pulling back the cover of her bed. She looked up and smiled. Joan smiled a trifle. "What are you doing?" she asked.

"Just getting everything ready, ma'am," the maid said with a smile.

"Ready?" Joan questioned. "Yes'm," the maid said. "I set out your night clothes and got the bed ready. While you were at dinner, the rest of your clothes came."

"The rest of my clothes?" Joan was perplexed. The maid went to a tall wardrobe and opened the door. Bright and light colors shimmered in the light of the candles about the room. There had to be at least twenty fine dresses hanging in that wardrobe. Joan gasped a little. "Good heavens, those aren't mine! I don't own that many dresses!"

The maid laughed then. She was a Black girl, dressed in a simple yet clean dark blue dress with a white apron, kerchief, and cap. "Your uncle bought them," she said with a smile.

"Uncle?" Joan said in surprise. "But why?"

The maid shrugged, then said, "You've got shoes too. And hats and bonnets." She smiled and pulled out a long drawer under the dresses. "And slippers and gloves." She was pulling out other drawers. She had all the drawers under the dresses opened.

"I can't even think of using that many things!" Joan cried in amazement.

"Look!" The maid beamed, heading for the bathroom. Joan followed. The maid went to the vanity table. She pulled out two drawers. "Ribbons!" She pulled out another drawer. "And jewelry!" Then she opened up yet another drawer. "And combs and brushes of every size, with pins." Then she pulled open another drawer. "These," she laughed, "are to curl and powder your hair." She waved toward the odd-shaped objects in the drawer. Joan shook her head in amazement. It was an hour before the maid, Jenny, had finished showing her everything her uncle had bought for her.

Chapter 14

The next day, Joan stood nervously at the window in the front parlor, dressed in a cream dress fringed with gold lace at the cuffs. It was slit down the front, elegantly showing a pretty petticoat of gold. Jenny had elegantly twisted and curled her hair on top of her head in a golden mass. Joan was uncomfortable, feeling stiff and top-heavy. Already her head ached. At the Hoods, she had always brushed her hair into one long braid and kept it down. Since she didn't ever leave the house, it was fine. She was definitely not accustomed to such a hairstyle as she was wearing now. Now she saw a fine and elegant carriage pull up in front of the house. The footman jumped down and opened the door. Three girls, dressed in fine silks ranging from seventeen to fifteen, descended and walked up the steps to the house. Joan slipped her crutch under her arm and went to stand in front of the fireplace. Her heart was flopping like a fish out of water, and she felt sick. The sooner this was over, the better!

"Miss Joan, the Fallo sisters," a maid said as she opened the door, and the three girls came in. The first, the one who looked fifteen, had bright and shimmering red hair combed atop her head in a style much like Joan's. She smiled. Her skin was a bit brown, and a spatter of freckles showed across her nose and cheeks.

She curtsied. "My name is Lisa Anna Fallo."

Joan smiled. The girl had a quiet voice and, in fact, she looked quiet. "How do you do?" Joan said softly, forcing her voice to remain calm because she was simply shaking with nervousness.

The next girl was the seventeen-year-old. She had black hair combed atop her head also. She was dressed in a bright and flashy red dress. "My name is Hannah Beth Fallo. Of course, I'm just delighted to meet you!" she gushed, dropping a curtsy primly.

Joan nodded, feeling a little sick. "I'm very glad to meet you too," she murmured.

The next was a girl about her own age. "I'm Diana Ethel Fallo," she said almost sharply. Her eyes flickered over Joan. "I'm glad to meet you."

Joan felt even more sick. "I'm glad you could come," she said. Then she waved a hand toward the chairs placed neatly about the tea table. "Please have a seat." The girls took their seats, and Joan limped forward and took hers also.

"When I heard Mr. Rindle had a niece, I just told Father I had to meet you!" Hannah Beth gushed, sitting down, and fluffing out her skirts. "You are so lucky to be the niece of such a wealthy man! Of course, I'm going to get into the family." She went on without taking a breath.

Joan raised an eyebrow imploringly. "What she means is marry Jeremiah," Diana Ethel said in a sharp voice. Joan was so shocked and surprised she burst out laughing. All three girls stared at her in amazement. Joan remembered the night before when the talk had turned to the Fallo girls.

"One's shy, one's always ornery, and the last forever talking," Jeremiah had said. "Lisa loves horses and is the shy one. Diana is snappish and will always try to make you feel uncomfortable. Hannah is just loud, annoying, and rude at times."

Joan choked back her laughter and began to pour the tea. "For someone with an unknown background, you are surprisingly gracious!" Hannah gushed. "Of course, I'm always better, but I am surprised!"

Joan only smiled. She had an idea. She turned to Lisa.

"Jeremiah tells me you love horses." Lisa's eyes lighted. "Yes," she said in a quiet voice.

"I like them but can't rightly ride. Also, I haven't done much with them," Joan said.

Lisa smiled. "They are beautiful creatures," she said, having lost her shyness, and continued. "I have a Palomino mare that came all the way from Spain. Papa gave her to me when I was thirteen. She was four at the time. She has had two colts since then. I don't ride her much. The one I ride most often is Kaddy. She's a black mare with a white stripe down her face." Joan smiled.

Hannah opened her mouth, but Lisa did not notice. She continued. "Papa just got a stallion." She rolled her eyes a little and sighed happily. "What a beauty! Completely white! He's huge! Papa has big hands, and he measured him. He stands nineteen hands high!" Joan couldn't help but whistle a little. "I know. You should see him when he starts acting up! He's murder! We have a special stall for him, padded and double-walled. Then we have a door that opens into another stall just the same. He will go in there. Then we slam the door and clean out the first stall. He's simply too big to do anything with!" Joan smiled, looking out the corner of her eye at Hannah and Diana.

"Well, I think that's enough talking about horses!" Hannah cut in. "Miss Rindle, have you seen the latest fashions?" Joan sighed a little and shook her head.

It was nearly an hour and a half when the three Fallo girls left. Then Joan was left alone. Totally exhausted, she put her arms on the tea table and her head in her arms. She felt dizzy and tired. "Joan?" She raised her head. Jamerson stood in the doorway to the parlor. "How was it?"

Joan shook·her head weakly. "I shall tell Uncle I don't want any more tea parties!" But even as she said it, she knew she wouldn't. Her uncle had been so kind, and she was going to do what he asked. Jamerson sat down opposite her. "I didn't have such a grand time today either. Uncle thought he should take me to see another one of his friends. He was a loyalist, and trying to keep politics out of it was the hardest thing I've ever done."

Joan smiled sympathetically. "You two look like you just ran a mile race," Jeremiah's voice suddenly boomed from the doorway.

"We feel like it," Jamerson said with a grin. Jeremiah grinned, walking over and flopping himself on a sofa.

"You're not used to people, are you?" he directed the question at Joan.

Joan shrugged, reaching for her crutch. "Just haven't been around them much." Then she said to Jamerson, "I'm going to go have a short rest. I feel completely exhausted!" Jamerson nodded, and Joan left the room.

A week passed. Joan and Jamerson's days just got busier and filled with more people. Besides the Fallo girls, Joan had to give tea parties to three other groups of sisters: the Kelps, the Gilos, and the Samersons. Mr. Rindle took Jamerson with him nearly every day to meet new people who consisted of Loyalists. At the end of the first week, Mr. Rindle presented Joan a pony and a small rig. These would be taken care of by a stable boy named Tim. Joan was greatly pleased. Now she would take quiet rides in the early morning, which often seemed to strengthen her for the coming day.

Another week came. On Saturday, Joan and Jamerson decided to take an all-day ride together and see the sights. This time, they decided to go down to the wharf and see their uncle's trading ships. They spent two or three hours getting tours of the massive vessels. There were nearly a dozen of them in the harbor that day. When they had toured the last one, Joan said, "Why don't we stop off at some tavern and get something to eat instead of going back?"

Jamerson grinned. "I say it sounds like a good idea."

He helped her into the rig and laid her crutch on the floor. "Tim, take us to a tavern. Make sure it's a good one, though. But not high-end," Jamerson called to the driver. The boy grinned and slapped the reins over the pony's back. They headed down the wharf.

Suddenly, Joan sat up straight and caught Jamerson's sleeve. "Look!" she cried, pointing. "That's the *Martha*!"

Jamerson grinned. "Tim, stop here." The rig stopped, and Jamerson and Joan watched as the cargo was unloaded. "Look, there's Captain," Jamerson said as a blue coat appeared. They waited until the cargo was unloaded, and then they saw Kurt come down the gangplank, a couple of sailors at his heels. "Kurt!" Jamerson called then. Kurt stopped and looked around. Joan and Jamerson waved.

For a moment, he stared at them, then walked slowly over. "What are you two doing in New York?" he asked, looking at them as though he expected to awaken from a dream any moment.

Joan laughed. "We'll tell you later. Get the captain, and we'll take you to dinner while we explain."

Kurt nodded and headed back aboard the *Martha*. A few minutes later, he returned with Captain Hood. The two got into the rig. "Back to our original plan, Tim," Jamerson called.

The rig started moving, and then Captain Hood asked, "So what's going on? What's with the fancy rig and clothes?"

Jamerson grinned. "I'll tell you over dinner."

Over the meal of roasted pheasant and boiled vegetables, Jamerson told the story.

"Whew!" Kurt whistled at last. "You're pretty rich."

"I wish we weren't," Joan murmured under her breath without thinking.

"Eh, what's that?" Captain Hood asked.

Joan blushed a little and shook her head. "Nothing."

Jamerson grinned. "You might think we love it, but we don't. I miss going to school with my friends and all. A little bit of work never hurt anybody, but Uncle thinks it does." Captain Hood frowned. "Also, he's a loyalist, and it's hard to get along with him." Kurt frowned. "Then why do you stay there?"

Jamerson shrugged. "Where else would we go?"

"Back home!" Captain Hood said.

"Oh, but we just butted into your family. Now that we got family, we couldn't expect you to continue to feed and clothe us. Especially when our uncle was one of the wealthiest men in England and now New York!"

"Poppycock!" Kurt said. "You're our family too now."

"That's right. You're like a son and daughter to me now," Captain Hood said. "If you want to go back, then by all means come back. We'd love to have you. But if you like the high life better, then we wish you happiness."

Joan and Jamerson looked at each other. "Jamerson can go back," Joan said quietly after a moment.

"What about you?" Kurt asked with a frown. "Well, I've never been much help since the fever, and I don't want anything I can't earn. With Uncle, he's my relation, and... well, there is just something different there."

The others looked at her worriedly. "Joan, we'd love to have you back," Captain Hood said quietly.

"You're a bigger help than you know, to Martha especially. With Kurt being gone and all, she's probably really lonely. If you came and kept her company, I'd be thankful."

Joan looked down. "I'll have to think about it."

"Well, I'm leaving!" Jamerson said. "Not staying here any longer!"

That night, Jamerson told Mr. Rindle, and the next morning he left on the *Martha*. Tim drove them all down to the wharf. They were silent. Joan felt a hard lump in her throat. Jamerson was leaving. Well, she really had to let him try his wings, and the Hoods would be good to him.

At the wharf, Captain Hood was the first one from the rig, and Jamerson was on his heels. "Be safe, Jamerson," Joan said to him. He grinned carefreely.

"I will. See you again." She knew he meant for her not to hear the last word, but she heard it as he turned away. "Maybe."

Kurt had got out. He turned to her. "He'll be fine, Joan. Don't worry. We'll bring him around as much as we can."

Joan nodded. "Give my regards to Martha," she said quietly.

Kurt nodded, bowed a little, then walked off.

A few minutes later, the gangplank was drawn in, and Jamerson called, "Bye, Joan!"

Joan waved. "Safe travels, Jamerson!" Then she turned to Tim. "Drive home."

Chapter 15

Joan sat under a large oak tree in her uncle's garden. The warm grass felt good under her touch, and the bushes were heavy with late flowers and roses. A lazy breeze shifted the branches overhead, stirring a curl across Joan's cheek. Joan sighed, looking up at the sky through the oak's branches. How long had it been since Jamerson had left? Two months. Now it was late August. "Miss Joan?"

Suddenly, a half-hearted voice called from down the path. Joan looked up. "Yes, Jenny?"

The maid hurried forward, something in her hand. "A messenger brought this to the house, ma'am, saying it was for you." Joan frowned a little in puzzlement but took the paper packet Jenny handed to her. The maid then left. Joan tore open the packet. Inside was a letter. Joan read:

Dear Joan,

Are you well? Do you like New York? Have you been getting enough to eat? I just can't help worrying because you are so much like a daughter to me. Jamerson is well and healthy. He's finishing up his school and will be leaving with James and Kurt next summer. Molly wishes for me to send you her best regards. She has been lonely since you left. It seems everyone who knew you hasn't been the same since you left. I must tell you, James was sorely troubled and saddened when you stayed in

New York. To him, you are like the daughter we lost so long ago. In fact, to me also in your way. But Eliza was Eliza, and you are you. Somehow, I must tell you about my daughter. She died in the way you got your leg crippled. So when you lived, I almost believed God had sent you to take her place in my aching heart. Also, to heal our family. When Eliza died, James took to sea, many times even in winter. Kurt was quiet and sad most of the time, and I couldn't really find ways to show my feelings. For those five years, Kurt was ten when Eliza died. Just a boy. I still regret how things were. But when you and Jamerson came, things changed. You helped me somehow. Maybe it was because I wanted to make you see I really wanted you to stay and be there as my daughter. When I saw how you were when you came. Quiet and shy. Never saying much and almost afraid to smile or show feelings, but caring oh so much for Jamerson. I knew that family was important, that Eliza hadn't been my only child. Also, somehow James wanted to stay home more. He spent the winter at home, like in the old days. I knew that in your naive way, you and Jamerson were healing our broken family. Now you have your own family. You have the money and luxuries you deserve. But dear Joan, please understand that you are always loved and wanted in our home. It does not matter to me if you are crippled or not. You do more than you shall ever know. I do not expect you to give up your new family or the money and friends you've made. I simply wanted to write. May God be with you in all you do.

With love,
Martha Hood

Joan leaned back against the trunk of the tree and sighed. Why must the Hoods act so? Didn't they understand that she couldn't be with them unless she could work her way? As she was placing Martha's letter back into the envelope, she saw another letter. She pulled it out.

Dear Joan,

Martha asked me to write, so I am. Things have been good here. Like always, the Hoods have been magnificent. Today, Kurt and Captain came into the harbor. Both were sorry to see you hadn't come back. Joan, why must you be so locked up? The Hoods are so good and love us both. I can't understand why you think you must earn your way with them. I can almost bet that you don't enjoy being there with Uncle. But you have your own strange ways. I've noticed that ever since we left London. I must say, I can't understand that, but then few boys ever understand their sisters. Anyways, Kurt asked me today what happened to us in London. He says he's been puzzling over it for some time. In fact, ever since we came to America. I told him to ask you if he ever got the chance because I don't remember much about it. Then he told me that if he did, he wouldn't find out anything because you are so quiet. "Sometimes it's maddening!" he told me. "It's as though nothing we can do can get to her. She's forever in a shell." I realized what he said was true because you are in a shell. Even to me. It's like you've locked yourself away and only you hold the key, which you do. Sometimes, I wish you would talk to me as you did in London and when we first came to America. But maybe that is too much to ask. I am your brother still. But different floats float different boats, you might say. Anyways, just like to say, we are all doing right good. I'll be out of school

*next summer and will be leaving with Kurt and
Captain.*

*Forever your loving brother,
Jamerson Rindle*

Joan shook her head. For a moment, she wanted to tear up the letter. Why didn't she talk to him as she once did? Because he had drawn away from her first. Somehow she knew that in time, he would tell the Hoods everything she had told him. She stuffed the letter back into the envelope and reached for her crutch. "Joan?" It was Jeremiah's voice.

"Coming," Joan called and rose unsteadily to her feet. Jeremiah came around a rose bush.

"There you are. Father is looking for you."

Joan nodded. "I'm on my way."

She went into the house and to her uncle's study. "There you are, my dear," Mr. Rindle said with a smile. "I have great news. My wife, who has been in England for the past six months, will arrive in two weeks. We must have the place ready, and I am counting on you to make sure the place is perfect. You'll have to check everything. The servants will do the cleaning. The housekeeper, Miss Peel, will help you. I'm leaving the details up to you."

Joan nodded. "Yes, sir. I shall do my best."

Chapter 16

"Alright," Joan said as she faced the hundred and fifty house servants, and the fifty yard workers and stable hands. "Mrs. Rindle shall be here in two weeks. The master wants everything to be perfect. Miss Peel and I will be on hand every hour of the day. Everything must be exactly perfect." She took a deep breath. "First, I want Miss Peel to make fourteen groups of the house servants, cooks not included, that work the best together." Miss Peel did. Then Joan said to the first group, "Now you ten will clean the top two floors, attic included. I don't want a speck of dust anywhere! Every rug must be taken out and shaken. All the drapes need to be taken down and washed and ironed. Not one window can have a speck on it. Every piece of furniture must be dusted and washed down with a damp cloth. Every fireplace cleaned out. Now, Miss Peel will inspect since I can't climb the stairs, and I don't want her to find even one speck of dust anywhere! Now you may be excused." From there, she continued. At last, she was to the last group. "Now I shall help you since you will be working on the first floor. I'll give orders as we go along." She gave a few short orders to get the group going, then turned to the cooks. "Now I want the finest meals and dishes planned for Mrs. Rindle's homecoming. The kitchen must be so clean that you would let the King of England lick off the floor." And she smiled a bit. "Not really, but it needs to be spotless." She turned to the head cook. "I'll talk over the menu with you later. Until then, put together all of Mrs. Rindle's favorite dishes." The cooks hurried away, and Joan turned to the yard workers and stable hands. She gave orders here too, short and to the point. Within ten minutes, servants were scurrying here and there. The whole house was abuzz. Joan worked just as hard as any of the servants.

The hubbub didn't stop until the very day that Mr. Rindle's biggest passenger ship sailed into the harbor, bearing on it the important Mrs. Rindle. Joan gave last-minute orders as her uncle hurried her out of the house to meet his wife. Jeremiah was there, dressed in a dark blue coat and breeches. His waistcoat was cream, and a frilly lace neckcloth. His tricorn matched his coat with a gold braid. Mr. Rindle was dressed somewhat the same, only in cream. Joan, though, was dressed in a coral-colored dress. Her hair elegantly topped her head, giving her a headache, and her feet fitted into a pair of silk slippers. At the wharf, Joan watched as the first-class passengers came off the ship. She was watching for an older woman, and perhaps that was the reason she was surprised when Mr. Rindle, who had gone to meet the passengers, walked up with a tall woman only in her late thirties. She was dressed fancier than Joan. Her eyes were dark brown, and her hair also. "Malinda, I'd like you to meet my long-lost grandniece," Mr. Rindle said, waving toward Joan.

The woman looked at Joan in surprise, then a bright and gentle smile touched her lips. "Yes, Jerry!" she said. "She does look indeed like Mary Vess! But she has John's eyes."

Joan looked at her in complete surprise. "Joan, I'd like you to meet my wife, Malinda."

Joan nodded a little. "I'm glad to meet you, Aunt Malinda," she said.

The woman laughed in gentle delight. "My word! I never did ponder what my name would sound like with an *Aunt* at the front of it." She smiled as she climbed into the carriage. She smiled at Jeremiah who had stayed in the carriage. "My goodness, Jeremiah, how you've grown, dear. Tell me, what have you been up to?"

Jeremiah grinned. "Just the usual, Mother. Looking after Father's business and helping out with business trips."

Aunt Malinda smiled. "It sounds like you've been busy." Jeremiah didn't say anything but shrugged a little. Mr. Rindle had gotten in, and now the carriage began to move.

*****

"I can't believe how well everything looks!" Mrs. Rindle said as she looked about her, while two manservants lugged a heavy trunk through the entry.

Mr. Rindle smiled as he placed a hand on Joan's shoulder. "I owe it all to Joan."

"Well done, Joan," Mrs. Rindle said with a smile.

"I didn't do anything, ma'am. The servants did all the work." The woman smiled and laughed a little.

"Come, dinner is ready," Mr. Rindle said, heading toward the dining room.

"Don't you think I should dress for dinner first?" Mrs. Rindle asked.

"Not this time," Mr. Rindle laughed.

In the dining room, the servants began to serve the meal. "I can't believe it! All my favorite dishes!" Mrs. Rindle said with a delighted smile.

"However did you manage all this?" she asked Joan. "You're just like your mother." Joan smiled, puzzled at how this woman knew her mother. "Everything is just perfect," Mrs. Rindle continued. "Jerry, I just don't know how you all managed it so nicely." Mr. Rindle chuckled.

"It was Joan, my dear. Give her all the credit." Mrs. Rindle smiled.

The next day, Joan was coming into the dining room when she heard low and angry voices unlike she had ever heard. "Gage can't do that!" She was surprised to hear Jeremiah's voice.

"Gage can, and he did!" This was her uncle's voice.

"He has no right taking our arms and powder!" Jeremiah said.

"He has the right, and God bless him for doing it!" Mr. Rindle snapped.

"He'll regret it. Believe me. He will! I hate him, and I hate the whole British army!" Jeremiah said, his voice rising.

"Boy, you are British!" Mr. Rindle said angrily.

"I know, and it's the biggest regret I can't fix. God knows how I wish I could!" Jeremiah snapped.

"How dare you speak so!" Mr. Rindle almost shouted. "You'll leave this house before you say one more word!"

"Very well, I shall!" There was a thud and a rattle of dishes, and then Jeremiah stormed out of the dining room. Joan flattened herself against the wall so he would not see her.

Mr. Rindle stormed out of the dining room after him, shouting, "You'll change your beliefs, boy, before you step foot in this house again!" Then he whirled around and saw her. "Joan!" he said in surprise.

Joan's eyes were wide with fright. "Uncle, you're not turning Jeremiah out, are you?"

"Yes!" bellowed her uncle.

"But, Uncle, he is your son!"

"And a traitor to England!" Joan stared at him. "Now let's have no more talk about it. When Malinda comes down, tell her I have gone for a walk!" Joan watched as her uncle stormed out of the house, then walked over and sat down on the stairs.

A few minutes later, Jeremiah came down the stairs dressed in a plain brown coat and breeches. Joan stood up. "Jeremiah, you can't leave," she said quietly.

He frowned a little. "Did you hear the argument?" Joan nodded. "Then you know I must go."

Joan sighed. "Then wait and say goodbye to your mother!"

"I already have," Jeremiah said as he headed for the door.

Joan followed on her crutch. "Then Godspeed wherever you go," she said.

He turned to look at her, then smiled. "Thank you. God bless you too, Joan. Goodbye."

Then he was gone, and Joan shook her head sadly. She heard footsteps behind her and looked around. Mrs. Rindle stood there. She looked hurriedly dressed. Her hair still hung about her shoulders.

"Is he gone?" she asked. Joan nodded.

"Dear me, I should have seen this coming," Mrs. Rindle said sorrowfully, sinking down on a step of the stairs.

It was two hours later when Mr. Rindle came back. "Malinda! Joan!" he called. Both women were in the parlor, waiting, and came hurriedly when he called.

"We're leaving for England at once!" Mr. Rindle said.

Joan gasped. "No!" she cried without warning.

"What's that?" Her uncle whirled on her.

"No, Uncle, please don't go to England!" Joan begged.

Her uncle frowned angrily. "Why not?" he asked. Joan bit her lip and looked down. A stubborn set came to her chin. "Why not?" her uncle demanded again.

"Because…" Joan started, then said quietly, "I belong to America."

Her uncle frowned angrily. "Go to your room at once!" he said.

Joan turned and went to her room. There, she sat down on her bed. She couldn't go to England. No, she *wouldn't* go to England! She frowned stubbornly and rose, limping to her desk. There, she scribbled a note reading:

Dear Jamerson,
Do the Hoods still want me? If they do, I shall come. Please write back as soon as possible.

Forever your loving and devoted sister,
Joan Anna Rindle

She folded it, then rang the bell that signaled Jenny. A few minutes later, Jenny came in. "Yes, ma'am?"

Joan passed her the piece of paper along with a silk purse filled with coins. "Take these to Tim. Tell him I want him to take this message to Jamerson at the Hood household. I have a map for him to go by here. Now tell him to hurry as fast as possible!" Jenny nodded, puzzled. Joan was watching out the window when Tim left the yard.

Joan sat reading in a chair by the window when there was a knock on the door. She raised her head. "May I come in?" Aunt Malinda asked, poking her head in.

Joan nodded. "Please," she murmured quietly.

The older woman came in and sat down on the edge of Joan's bed. "Jerry is sorely upset," she said quietly. "Not only by our son's actions but yours also." Joan looked down in defiance. She wouldn't go to England! "Now please understand what I am saying," Mrs. Rindle said. "Things have been hard for Jerry. All these years searching for you and your brother. When I met him, I was only sixteen. He was in his late thirties. We met in England, but I was born in Switzerland." Joan frowned a bit but listened. "I was the cousin of your mother. Jerry did not know that until later though. We were married when I was seventeen. Your mother, being several years younger, was married later. Jerry didn't find out about your mother's and my relationship until I told him when he was searching for your father. Then I told him I knew exactly where they lived, though I hadn't contacted them in some time. That's when we found out about their death and you and your brother running away. We searched London for a very long time until one day when your father's older sister sent a message to me saying that she was dying and had a matter of great importance to tell me. There, on her deathbed, she told me about a Captain Hood who had come to England looking for your parents, and by some miracle, she had heard of him. She said she gave him some of your parents' belongings she had saved."

Joan was staring at her aunt in amazement. "Then you knew my mother?" she asked.

"Yes, child. Indeed, I did," Aunt Malinda said with a smile. "Your personality is a lot like hers. Quiet and not saying much. But I have to admit, you are quieter than Mary Vess ever was." Joan looked down. "Now listen to me, Joan. This matter about England

and America, feel it carefully before you choose. But you must feel it is the right decision before you decide. Now think about it." Joan nodded mutely, and her aunt left the room.

Chapter 17

A month passed, and the Rindle household was abuzz as everybody was readying for the move to England. Joan waited for the return letter from Jamerson. Meanwhile, she helped all she could. She knew she had made the decision Aunt Malinda had been talking about long ago. After a month, she began to expect Tim to be back. Each night she asked Jenny if the stable boy had returned. It was three or four days before the family would leave for England when Jenny entered Joan's room just as Joan was about to blow out the candle after a long day. "Ma'am?" she said in a cautious voice. "Tim is back with a message."

Joan was out of bed in an instant. "Where is it? Pass it here." Jenny handed her a piece of paper. It read:

> *Dear Joan,*
>
> *Of course, the Hoods still want you! They always have. They wish for you to come at once. Martha sent her love and says she can hardly wait. I can hardly wait to see you. Now Captain is back, and he is sick, as are the rest of us. Not badly, so do not worry. He is sending Rudy Winn for you in a little skiff that his father owns. He will have brought your messenger to New York. I have given him directions to Uncle's house. From there, you shall get further instructions.*
>
> *Your brother,*
> *Jamerson Rindle*

Joan looked up at Jenny and smiled. "Thank you. Good night."

The very next morning, Joan was packing heavy books from her uncle's library when a maid came hurrying in. "Ma'am, there is a gentleman here to see you." Joan nodded and slipped her crutch under her arm. "He's in the front parlor," the maid said, and Joan nodded again.

Joan recognized the young man the instant she came in as one of Jamerson's friends from long ago. He bowed a little. "Miss Rindle, I presume?" he said.

Joan nodded. "I'm guessing you are Mr. Winn," she said.

"Indeed, ma'am. Your brother and Captain Hood asked me if I could come and get you."

Joan nodded again. "Yes, he sent a message. Now tell me, is Jamerson alright?" she asked anxiously.

Rudy Winn nodded. "Yes, ma'am, still a touch weak from the sickness but fine."

Joan sighed with relief, then said, "I want to make one thing clear. My family is not to know about my leaving. Simply come by tonight after all lights are out, and I'll be waiting."

The young man nodded, bowing again. "Bring something warm," he said. "The weather is quite nippy."

"I shall. Good day, Mr. Winn." He bowed again and left. Joan sighed. She couldn't believe she was leaving New York. She would be seeing Jamerson again.

Joan glanced at the letter in her hand and sighed. It was the best she could do. She read it over once more.

> *Dear Uncle Jeremiah and Aunt Malinda,*
> *Please don't get me wrong. I've tried to think*
> *that perhaps I would change after so long, but I can-*
> *not. America has become my home, and I couldn't*
> *bear to leave it. Freedom means more to me than*
> *wealth or life. Thank you for being oh-so-good to*

me. I shall be in good hands, never fear. May God keep you in the hollow of his hand forever and ever.

Forever your loving and devoted niece,
Joan Anna Rindle

Joan sighed quietly and turned toward her bag with all the clothes she had brought. Well, she hoped they would understand. She struggled to get her bag and crutch to work together then blew out the candle and opened the door. Her crutch sounded very loud as she went down the hall. A few minutes later, she lifted the bolt off the front door, hobbled through, then closed the door behind her. As she turned, she saw a small buggy come out of the shadows and pull almost noiselessly up to the steps. Rudy Winn jumped out and came up the steps. He took her bag and helped her down the steps and into the buggy. Then the buggy pulled away, and Joan only looked back once. At the wharf, Rudy Winn showed her to a neat little sloop moored to the wharf. He helped her aboard, then said, "Stay right here. I'll be back. I got to run the buggy back to the stable where I rented it." Joan nodded, pulling her cloak more firmly about her. It was less than twenty minutes before he returned. The wind was strong and nippy. Rudy Winn adjusted the sail, then cast off from the wharf. Joan watched through the gathering fog and darkness as the New York harbor slipped away and at last disappeared. Then she turned her face into the wind and breathed a sigh of pleasure and relief.

Joan awoke in a small bunk. She lay there for a moment, staring above her, trying to recall where she was. Then it all came flooding back. She remembered Rudy Winn's help to get her below decks, and then she found the small and neat cabin and slipped into the bunk. She sat up and yawned a little. She found her bag where it had slid under the bed, dressed, and combed her hair, feeling delighted at once again being dressed in the simple garments Martha had made for her. Once again, she felt a little scared about going back. She went to the door of her cabin and peeked out. The boat was silent, and she went out, her crutch not being very stable on the rocking boat. She found the main cabin where Rudy Winn sat studying some maps and charts. He looked up and smiled a little.

"Good morning." Joan nodded. "I made some breakfast," Rudy said, nodding toward some bread and cheese on a plate that slid back and forth across the table. Joan sat down and ate, wondering how much she would have to pay this man for taking her home.

At last, she asked, "How'd Jamerson get sick?"

"Something he caught from the captain and Kurt when they came off their last voyage." Joan frowned a little but said nothing.

"He'll be fine," Rudy said. "He was almost better when Tommy and I left." Joan didn't bother to ask who Tommy was but nodded. The days seemed slow for Joan, and she stayed below deck. But at last, one day Rudy came below grinning. "Ma'am," he said, "we're pulling into the harbor!"

Joan gasped and looked up in amazement. "You mean…?"

Rudy Winn smiled. "Better get your things."

Joan nodded, and she never moved so fast on her crutch as she did then. She gathered her things quickly together, and then Rudy Winn helped her on deck, and Joan saw that they were indeed pulling into the familiar harbor she had come into three years before and pulled out of six months earlier. She could see a group waiting on the wharf. Suddenly, Joan felt nervous. Did the Hoods really want her? Was Jamerson speaking the truth when he had said they did? Before she could make more doubts, the boat bumped the wharf, and a tall young man jumped aboard. Joan was shocked. "Jamerson!"

His looks and manner were nothing like she had remembered. She had left him a boy, and now he stood before her almost a man. Jamerson chuckled. "Hi, Joan, I'm glad you came back."

"How do you feel? Mr. Winn said you were sick when he left."

Jamerson grinned. "Fine as a fiddle now." Joan then saw the Hoods in the background. Kurt had grown again. He was taller. Captain Hood stood beside him, looking a bit small beside his strapping son. Martha stood next to them; her face lit with delight. One look at it told Joan that the Hoods truly did want her.

Happily, Joan settled back into the life she knew and loved. She missed her uncle, of course, but she was glad to be back. At first, she seemed even more shy than at first, but soon she was her usual self. It was as though nothing had ever happened.

Chapter 18

It was April 29, 1775. Joan stood at the window, watching for Jamerson and Kurt. The *Martha* was pulling out late that year. Suddenly, Joan caught sight of the two boys running up the street. She knew something was wrong and reached hurriedly for her crutch. She heard the front door bang, and Jamerson yelled, "Joan?" Joan was in the entry in a moment. "Pack us some food." Joan stared at him.

"What for?"

Jamerson and Kurt looked at each other. "The war has started," Kurt said. She knew he was trying to speak solemnly, but his eyes danced with excitement, and his hands shook a little.

"Oh!" gasped Joan, her eyes widening in surprise and her own pulse quickened with excitement.

"You just can't go!" Martha cried, frowning at the two boys.

"Ma, please," Kurt said. "I'm eighteen now, and Jamerson is fifteen. I'll take good care of him."

Martha shook her head. "No! No! A thousand times no!" Tears filled her eyes.

The two boys looked at each other, and then Kurt cleared his throat. "Then at least wish us health before we leave."

Joan stood off to one side, watching the faces of the two serious young men. Yes, nothing was going to interfere with their patriotism to their country. Martha stared at Kurt, then a sob caught in her throat, and she said in a voice barely above a whisper, "Yes, God be with you. May he hold you in the hollow of his hand and protect you in all you do and may you return home safely in body and soul."

Then she turned swiftly away and walked into the kitchen. The boys turned to Joan.

Joan smiled. "May God be with you wherever you go," she said quietly, in a tone that voiced that the blessing came from her heart.

Jamerson smiled and stepped forward. "Don't worry, Joan, I'll write whenever I can." Then he hugged her and turned to Captain Hood, who stood back. "Well, sir, I guess things have changed, eh?

The captain nodded. "I'd join you two boys myself, but I'm getting on in years, and the ladyfolk need someone to look after them." He shook the two boys' hands, then said, "Well, give them Redcoats something to remember."

"Aye-Aye, sir," Kurt said with a grin, and Jamerson smiled. Then they shouldered their packs and left the house. Joan followed them onto the porch and watched until their figures disappeared down the road.

*****

Joan sat numbly by the window, staring at the falling rain. How many weeks since Jamerson had left? Four. He had written, and she held the unopened letter in her hand. Somehow she felt afraid of what lay in the letter. Slowly, she opened it and read:

> *Dear Joan,*
>
> *I do hope this letter finds you in good health. How is everyone? It seems Kurt and I have been walking for eternity! I would tell you what plans are being made by our leader, but it is top secret. Instead, I will tell you about our trip. It has been mostly good weather, though my feet feel as though they would surely fall off! The places we have passed are unique, beautiful, unpleasant, and most common in turn. Kurt is well and wishes me to ask you to let Martha read the next verse.*
>
> *Dear Ma,*

Joan looked up at Martha and held out the letter. "Here's news from Kurt. Read it, would you, please? My eyes aren't as sharp as they used to be," Martha said. Joan nodded.

Dear Ma,

Never worry about me. Things aren't as bad as they are to be expected. We are traveling in a group. The food is alright, though a little skimpy. I can't believe we are actually in a real war with England. How is Father? Has he set out to sea yet? I'm sure he has. I have to admit, I am homesick, but never fear. May God bless you always,

Your forever devoted son,
Kurt Hood

Martha smiled as tears filled her eyes. "He is frank, and I do worry about him, but I guess freedom has its price too."

January 27, 1776. Joan stared blankly at the letter in her hand. Her heart had stopped as she read the shaky handwriting.

Dear Joan,

Kurt is wounded! I have hired a man to bring him home. I managed to escape from the British. I must say, our attack on the city of Quebec met with a sorry retreat, and many of my comrades were taken prisoner, and some were killed. When the war started, I thought it would be fun and mostly a game. I have witnessed that it is not. Never worry about me. I made it out fine, but I have realized what war means, as did Kurt. He will not die, I don't think, but he does need a couple of months of recuperation. Please try not to make Martha wor-

ried. Break the news gently and try to keep her as worry-free as possible.

> *Heaven's angels be with you,*
> *Jamerson Rindle*

Joan covered her mouth with a shaking hand for a minute, as though to stop her own nervousness and to hold back the hysterical worry that pushed into her mind and heart. Then she slowly folded the letter and looked up at Captain Hood, who had brought the letter. "What is it?" the captain asked.

Joan took a deep breath. "Kurt has been wounded. The attack on Quebec failed, and Jamerson is sending him home to heal."

The captain's face paled. "Is he bad?"

Joan shook her head. "Jamerson thinks he will not die." The captain ran a shaking hand across his face and nodded.

It was a month later when a sorry-looking cart pulled up to the Hood's doorstep, and the driver said he had one Kurt Hood. Captain Hood went to help bring his son in. The company room had been made into a bedroom. Kurt was carried in and laid on the bed. Joan followed with towels and a basin of warm water. "Where were you hit, son?" Captain Hood asked.

"The belly," Kurt muttered.

"What?" Martha gasped. "It's a wonder you are not dead!"

Kurt groaned a little. "Ma, don't worry. If I have lived this long…I will recover." His face was ashen, and he looked very tired.

"Let's get the wound cleaned, and then we'll let you rest," Captain Hood said gently. Joan passed the hot water and towels to him and went to fetch fresh bandages. Her heart felt tight. Would this happen to Jamerson sometime? Where was he?

*****

Joan sat at the spinning wheel; her head swarmed with worry over Jamerson. "Joan?" Joan looked up as the back door opened, and Molly stuck her head in.

"Oh, hi, Molly," Joan said.

Molly came in. "I heard Kurt arrived today." Joan nodded. "Where was he wounded?"

"The stomach."

"The stomach?" Molly gasped. "No one can live with a stomach wound!"

"Well, he has lived so far, and I believe he will continue to live."

"But a stomach wound?" Molly said.

Joan bit her lip. "I know, Molly. Don't ask me how he lived so far, but he has."

Molly looked at her closely. "Worried about Jamerson?" Joan looked up and shrugged a little.

"Every girl worries about her brother when he's away at war."

"Yes," Molly said quietly. "I suppose they do."

Joan peeked in the company room door. "Awake?" she asked quietly as Kurt turned his head to look at her.

"I guess I am," he said.

Joan came in. "I brought you some dinner."

"Let me guess. Gruel?"

"Well, that's all you can eat at the moment," Joan said, setting the tray on the nightstand.

"I suppose it is," Kurt muttered.

"How do you feel?" Joan asked.

Kurt shrugged a little. "As good as to be expected of a man with a belly wound."

Joan smiled. "Oh, by the way," she laughed suddenly, standing up. "I got you a birthday present." She went out for a moment and returned, struggling to hold a bulky wrapped object and her crutch at the same time. She passed the object to Kurt. "Be careful. It's heavy, and you're still weak," she said.

Kurt unwrapped the paper and stared at the object in amazement. "Where'd you get a British musket?"

Joan smiled. "It doesn't matter."

Kurt looked at her. "No, really."

Joan laughed. "That is a secret."

Kurt shook his head, looking back at the musket in his hands. "I can't believe this!"

Joan smiled. "Now when you go back, you have to let Jamerson shoot it."

Kurt chuckled. "Oh, I will." Joan smiled and left the room.

*****

Spring dawned bright and cheery, and Kurt was able to be up and about a little. Captain Hood was readying his ship when news reached town. The Continental Congress had declared that all American ports were open to ships from all countries besides England. This did not bother anyone in town because the ship captains in town had long stopped shipping from England. The day the news arrived, Joan was in the kitchen making little tea cakes for Molly. Kurt sat at the window, reading. Suddenly, he asked, "Joan, what happened to you in England?"

Joan raised her head and looked at him. "Whatever do you mean?" she asked quietly.

"Yes, I mean what made you so quiet and shy, so…so untrusting?"

Joan brushed back a curl from her cheek with her shoulder and sighed quietly.

"Really, Kurt, I wish you wouldn't ask."

"But I must!" Kurt said. "I have been silent for four long years. I've waited, hoping you'd tell me. Jamerson has told me all he can remember, but I know there is more to what he says!"

Joan placed the cakes in the small oven in the hearth and turned toward him. "I have left that part of my life in the past," she said quietly.

"Not all of it," Kurt said. "You are still quiet and don't say much. You never really speak of yourself."

Joan shrugged. "It doesn't matter."

"But it does, Joan. Really, truly to me, it does!"

Joan sighed and washed her hands in a basin of water and shook her head.

"Kurt," she said a little impatiently.

"Joan, I must know!"

Joan looked at him for a moment then walked over, picked up the mending basket, and sat down in a chair near the table. Then she told her story, halting every now and again. Kurt listened to the story. To think anyone had gone through so much at such a young age. The poverty and drudgery. Every obstacle she had faced and overcome. It seemed impossible, yet she had. At last, Joan stood up. "That is it. Now you know, and now you must carry it to the grave."

Kurt nodded solemnly, and he knew he would.

The next week, Kurt left, and the war went on. Joan seemed more peaceful since she had told her story and unlocked the deep hurt in her soul. She was different, happier, and ready to trust. Martha and Captain Hood at last found the daughter they had so long waited for, and Joan found the security she had always longed for.

The End

Afterword

If you are a person who likes to know what happens to characters after a book ends, then this is for you. Joan Anna Rindle was married to an American patriot, Nathaniel Kelp, on August 25, 1776. Together they had four children. Joan lived into her late nineties and died the same year as her husband. Jamerson Rindle was wounded on April 8, 1780, in the Bombardment of Fort Moultrie in South Carolina. Later the same year, he was married to Angela Pin. Kurt Hood sadly died in the winter of 1777 at Valley Forge, also known as the Winter of Red Snow. He was engaged at the time to Molly Deeks, who later married a sailor, Josh Conn. Martha and Captain Hood managed to live through the war and witness the founding of the United States of America. Jeremiah Rindle Senior moved back to England with his wife and never returned to America. Sadly, he never again spoke to his son. Matters were left as Joan had seen them. Jeremiah Rindle served throughout the war as a scout for Colonel Francis Marion. Sadly, he too died, only two days after Cornwallis surrendered at Yorktown, Virginia, in 1781. But the memory of all those who died still lives on in the minds of the brave Americans who remember the sacrifice that was made to make this country free.\

About the Author

Frances Mary was born in Utah. At age nine, her family moved to Denver, Colorado, where Frances became greatly interested in books and reading. At age ten, she began to write short stories. Frances was homeschooled her entire school life, along with her eleven siblings. Her writing was greatly inspired by famous author Frances Hodgson Burnett, author of *The Secret Garden* and *Little Lord Fauntleroy*. When she was eleven, Frances Mary printed a newspaper for her family which would come out every week. Through it, she finished several short stories. Later, at age thirteen, she began to write seriously and looked for a chance to publish her work. Her greatest support team came from her family, who thought her dream of becoming a published author could happen. Frances wrote stories mainly for her younger siblings, many of her characters were actually molded to get reactions from her young sisters. Her best friend and cousin, who studied art, painted many of Frances's characters. Her first book, *The English Rebels*, was published when she was sixteen. Frances's main point in writing the book was, as she told her siblings, "To show young people what people of those times went through for our freedom, and what they gave up for what many believed was just a mere dream."